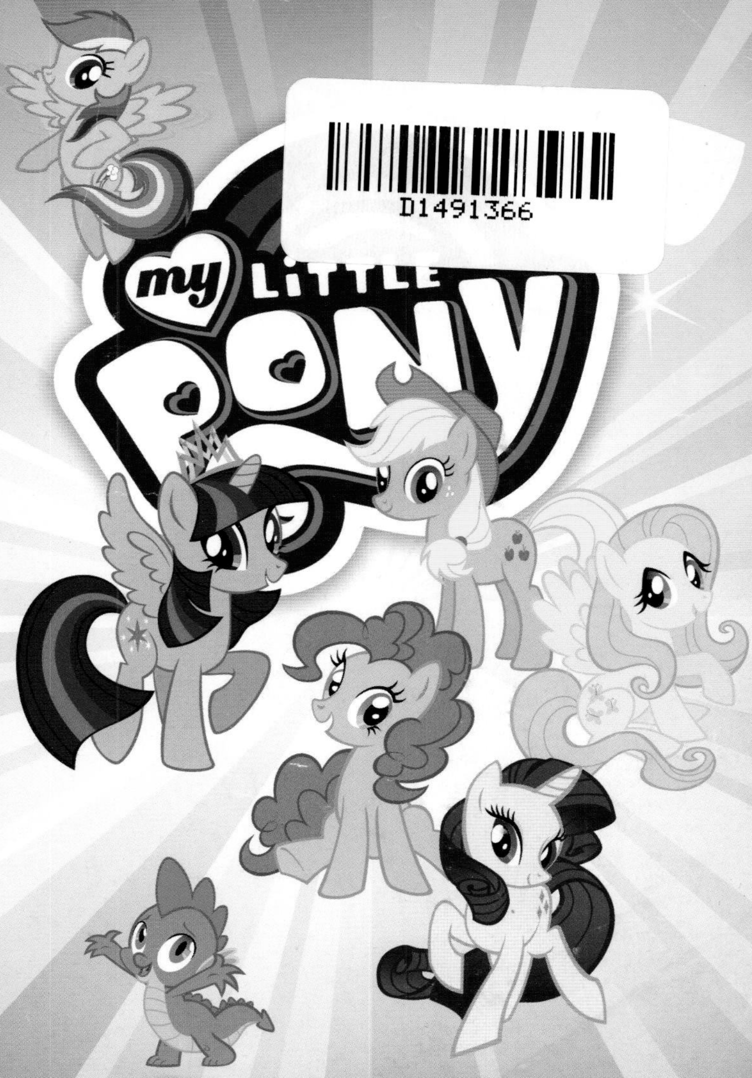
my LITTLE PONY

Shadowplay

Special thanks to Ed Lane, Beth Artale, and Michael Kelly.

ISBN: 978-1-68405-755-9
24 23 22 21   1 2 3 4

Nachie Marsham, Publisher
Rebekah Cahalin, EVP of Operations
Blake Kobashigawa, VP of Sales
John Barber, Editor-in-Chief
Justin Eisinger, Editorial Director, Graphic Novels and Collections
Scott Dunbier, Director, Special Projects
Anna Morrow, Sr. Marketing Director
Tara McCrillis, Director of Design & Production
Mike Ford, Director of Operations
Shauna Monteforte, Sr. Director of Manufacturing Operations

Ted Adams and Robbie Robbins, IDW Founders

Licensed By:

www.IDWPUBLISHING.com

My Little Pony

Shadowplay

Story by
Josh Haber

Adaptation by
Justin Eisinger

Lettering and Design by
Nathan Widick

Edits by
Alonzo Simon & Zac Boone

MEET THE PONIES

Twilight Sparkle

TWILIGHT SPARKLE TRIES TO FIND THE ANSWER TO EVERY QUESTION! WHETHER STUDYING A BOOK OR SPENDING TIME WITH PONY FRIENDS, SHE ALWAYS LEARNS SOMETHING NEW!

Spike

SPIKE IS TWILIGHT SPARKLE'S BEST FRIEND AND NUMBER ONE ASSISTANT. HIS FIRE BREATH CAN DELIVER SCROLLS DIRECTLY TO PRINCESS CELESTIA!

Applejack

APPLEJACK IS HONEST, FRIENDLY AND SWEET TO THE CORE! SHE LOVES TO BE OUTSIDE, AND HER PONY FRIENDS KNOW THEY CAN ALWAYS COUNT ON HER.

Fluttershy

FLUTTERSHY IS A KIND
AND GENTLE PONY WITH A
BIG HEART. SHE LIKES TO
TAKE CARE OF OTHERS,
ESPECIALLY HER LITTLE
ANIMAL FRIENDS.

Rarity

RARITY KNOWS HOW
TO ADD SPARKLE TO
ANY OUTFIT! SHE LOVES
TO GIVE HER PONY
FRIENDS ADVICE ON THE
LATEST FASHIONS AND
HAIRSTYLES.

Rainbow Dash

RAINBOW DASH LOVES TO FLY AS FAST AS SHE CAN! SHE IS ALWAYS READY TO PLAY A GAME, GO ON AN ADVENTURE, OR HELP OUT ONE OF HER PONY FRIENDS.

Starlight Glimmer

STARLIGHT GLIMMER IS A POWERFUL UNICORN AND TWILIGHT SPARKLE'S PUPIL. ONCE CONVINCED THAT PONIES SHOULD SURRENDER THEIR CUTIE MARKS TO IMPROVE FRIENDSHIP, HER ADVENTURES WITH TWILIGHT HAVE TAUGHT HER OTHERWISE.

Pinkie Pie

PINKIE PIE KEEPS HER
PONY FRIENDS LAUGHING
AND SMILING ALL DAY!
CHEERFUL AND PLAYFUL,
SHE ALWAYS LOOKS ON
THE BRIGHT SIDE.

Sunburst

SUNBURST IS AN INSIGHTFUL
ROYAL CRYSTALLER TO
FLURRY HEART. EVER
SINCE TWILIGHT SPARKLE
HELPED HIM RECONNECT
WITH CHILDHOOD FRIEND
STARLIGHT, HE HAS CALLED
THE CRYSTAL EMPIRE HOME.

Shadowplay

SOMEWHERE IN EQUESTRIA.

THE BEST ELEMENTS WITHIN US...

FLIPPP

...CAN SPREAD LIGHT AND VIRTUE.

AND I KNOW PONIES WHO REPRESENT THEM ALL...

BEAUTY

STRENGTH

SORCERY

HEALING

HOPE

BRAVERY

MYSELF, AND THESE *PILLARS OF EQUESTRIA* WERE GATHERED TOGETHER...

...BY *ANOTHER* TO MAINTAIN AND SHARE THE LIGHT OF THESE POWERFUL IDEALS.

BUT WE SOON CAME TO BELIEVE THE PONY WHO BROUGHT US TOGETHER...

...ONLY WANTED THAT POWER FOR *HIMSELF.*

CAST OUT AND ALONE...

...THIS POWER-MAD PONY TURNED TO DARKNESS TO SATISFY HIS THIRST.

TRANSFORMED INTO A PONY OF SHADOWS...

...HE RETURNED FOR REVENGE...

...TO EXTINGUISH THE PILLARS OF LIGHT AND ROB THE WORLD OF HOPE.

TO STOP HIM, THE PILLARS AND I MUST MAKE A GRAVE SACRIFICE.

BUT WE SHALL LEAVE BEHIND A SEED...

...IN HOPES THAT ONE DAY IT WILL *GROW* INTO A FORCE...

...TO STAND AGAINST THE DARKNESS FOR ALL TIME.

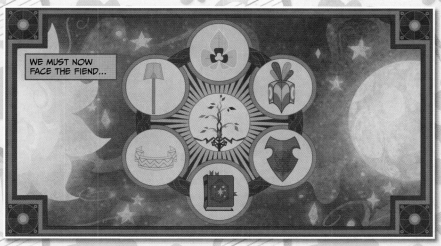

WE MUST NOW FACE THE FIEND...

...WITH THE ONLY PLAN WE HAVE.

"...I ONLY HOPE IT WILL BE ENOUGH."

THAT'S THE LAST ENTRY.

AND MAYBE STARSWIRL'S FINAL WORDS BEFORE HE *VANISHED!*

GAH!

WAH?

I'VE ALWAYS WONDERED WHAT HAPPENED TO STARSWIRL.

THIS IS QUITE A DISCOVERY, SUNBURST.

I AM HAPPY TO ASSIST.

SO IT'S GENUINE?

YOU CAN VERIFY THAT THIS JOURNAL REALLY DID BELONG TO *STARSWIRL THE BEARDED?!*

INDEED.

AND FROM THE LOOKS OF IT...

...THE LAST THING HE WROTE BEFORE FACING THE *PONY OF SHADOWS.*

HUH?!

UH... SO, THE PONY OF SHADOWS WAS REALLY *REAL?*

WE NEVER MET THE OTHER PILLARS...

...AND WERE TOO YOUNG TO UNDER-STAND THE DANGER THEY FACED.

IT APPEARS SO.

HOLD ON A SECOND. ALL THOSE LEGENDARY PONIES WERE ALL REAL TOO?

AND THEY WENT OFF WITH STARSWIRL TO FACE THE PONY OF SHADOWS.

AND THEN *NONE* OF THEM WERE EVER HEARD FROM AGAIN?

AH... YEAH. WEREN'T YOU LISTENING?

BUT WHAT HAPPENED TO THEM ALL?

THEY MUST HAVE DEFEATED THE VILLAIN, SINCE *EQUESTRIA* IS STILL FULL OF LIGHT AND HOPE.

BUT HOW? AND WHERE DID THEY GO?

MY OLDE PONISH IS A BIT RUSTY...

...BUT I WONDER IF THE ANSWERS CAN BE FOUND SOMEWHERE WITHIN THE PAGES OF THIS BOOK.

WELL, I JUST HAPPEN TO BE AN **EXPERT**...

...IN OLDE PONISH.

I MEAN, I'VE PRACTICALLY MEMORIZED...

...EVERY ANCIENT TEXT ABOUT STARSWIRL THERE IS!

SERIOUSLY. **ALL** OF THEM.

WE HAVE FOND MEMORIES OF OUR OLD TEACHER.

IF YOU COULD DISCOVER WHAT HAPPENED TO HIM, WE WOULD BE MOST GRATEFUL.

OF COURSE!

SOLVING A THOUSAND-YEAR-OLD MYSTERY COULD TAKE FOREVER!

THINK OF THE RESEARCH, THE RE-READING...

...THE *RE-RE-READING*...

YOU MIGHT FIND YOU NEED HELP.

LUCKILY, SHE'S GOT A WHOLE *BUSHEL* OF HELPERS RIGHT HERE.

TOTALLY!

UM... HOW LONG WILL ALL THIS RESEARCH TAKE, EXACTLY?

LET'S GET THIS BACK TO MY LIBRARY.

I'M SURE WE'LL FIGURE OUT WHAT HAPPENED IN NO TIME.

HOORAY!

YEAH!

LET'S GO!

LATER...

FSSSHHHHH

YAWWW...

FIGURE IT OUT YET, TWILIGHT?

WHAT?

YOU FIGURED IT OUT?!

WHAT IS IT?

NOTHING. I MEAN, STARSWIRL WAS A GENIUS, OBVIOUSLY...

...BUT FORGET OLDE PONISH...

...THERE'S PARTS WHERE HIS *HORNWRITING* IS LIKE ANOTHER LANGUAGE!

TWILIGHT, WE'VE BEEN STUDYIN'...

...AND REFERENCIN'...

...AND CROSS REFERENCING FOR THREE DAYS STRAIGHT NOW.

YEAH.

I HAVEN'T SPENT THIS MUCH TIME READING...

...SINCE THE LAST DARING DO BOOK CAME OUT.

PERHAPS IT'S TIME TO TAKE A BREAK.

THIS MYSTERY IS A THOUSAND YEARS OLD, AFTER ALL...

...ANOTHER DAY OR TWO WON'T MAKE A DIFFERENCE.

TWO DAYS?!

I DON'T WANT TO WASTE TWO SECONDS.

I'M CLOSE TO AN ANSWER. I CAN FEEL IT.

"HEARG SYLFUM...

"...SE PONEHENGE."

WHAT'S THAT?!

THE TEMPLE OF **PONEHENGE?!**

YOU CAN READ *THAT?*

THE *HORNWRITING'S* PRETTY SLOPPY...

...BUT IT'S NOWHERE NEAR AS BAD AS MINE.

"TOWARD DOL GRIMLIC OF FOLA FIRGENBEORG?"

I... I'M NOT SURE...

AT THE BASE OF FOAL MOUNTAIN...

"...USER ENDEMEST SCIELD..."

GAH!

OUR LAST STAND!

WELL, THAT SURE SOUNDS LIKE A CLUE TO ME.

VVRRRRNNN

I THINK I FOUND SOMETHING.

LOOK!

MOMENTS LATER...

VVRRRRRNNN

THIS IS IT!

PONEHENGE. I CAN'T BELIEVE IT.

VVURRRNNN

HEY WHAT'S THAT?

I'VE NEVER SEEN MAGICAL RUNES LIKE THESE BEFORE.

HAVE YOU?

NUH-UH.

I DON'T THINK ANYPONY'S SEEN ANY OF THIS FOR A LONG TIME.

26

YOU'RE RIGHT.

I'M NOT SURE WE'LL FIND OUT WHAT HAPPENED HERE A THOUSAND YEARS AGO.

I SUPPOSE IT WAS A LONG SHOT.

CHEER UP, TWILIGHT.

FINDING A WHOLE SET OF ANCIENT RUNES IS PRETTY IMPRESSIVE.

YOU COULD WRITE A PAPER ON IT!

I GUESS I HOPED WE'D GET HERE...

...AND THE MYSTERY WOULD JUST MAGICALLY BE EXPLAINED.

ZXZXZXZRRRNNNN

AH... TWILIGHT?

ZXZXZXZRRRNNNN

UMMMM...

STARSWIRL?!

IS IT YOU?

I'VE WANTED TO MEET YOU MY WHOLE LIFE.

I CAN'T BELIEVE YOU'RE HERE!

ZX-ZX-ZX-ZX-ZRRRRNNNN

SUNBURST'S HOOF PASSES RIGHT THROUGH THE GLOWING BODY...

I DON'T THINK HE IS HERE.

I DON'T THINK ANY OF THEM ARE!

WHA—

ALL AROUND, THE *PILLARS OF EQUESTRIA* HAVE APPEARED!

TWILIGHT, WHAT'S GOING ON?!

VVRRRRNNN

SUNBURST THINKS—

ZXORT!

GWAH!

ZXZXZXRRNNNN

SWIK

WHUMP

WHUMP

RAWRL!

BWAH HA HA HA

YOU SUMMON ME AT YOUR PERIL, STARSWIRL.

ONCE I DEFEAT ALL OF YOU...

...THIS REALM WILL EMBRACE THE DARKNESS...

...AS I DID SO LONG AGO.

AND NOW...

FWUNK!

32

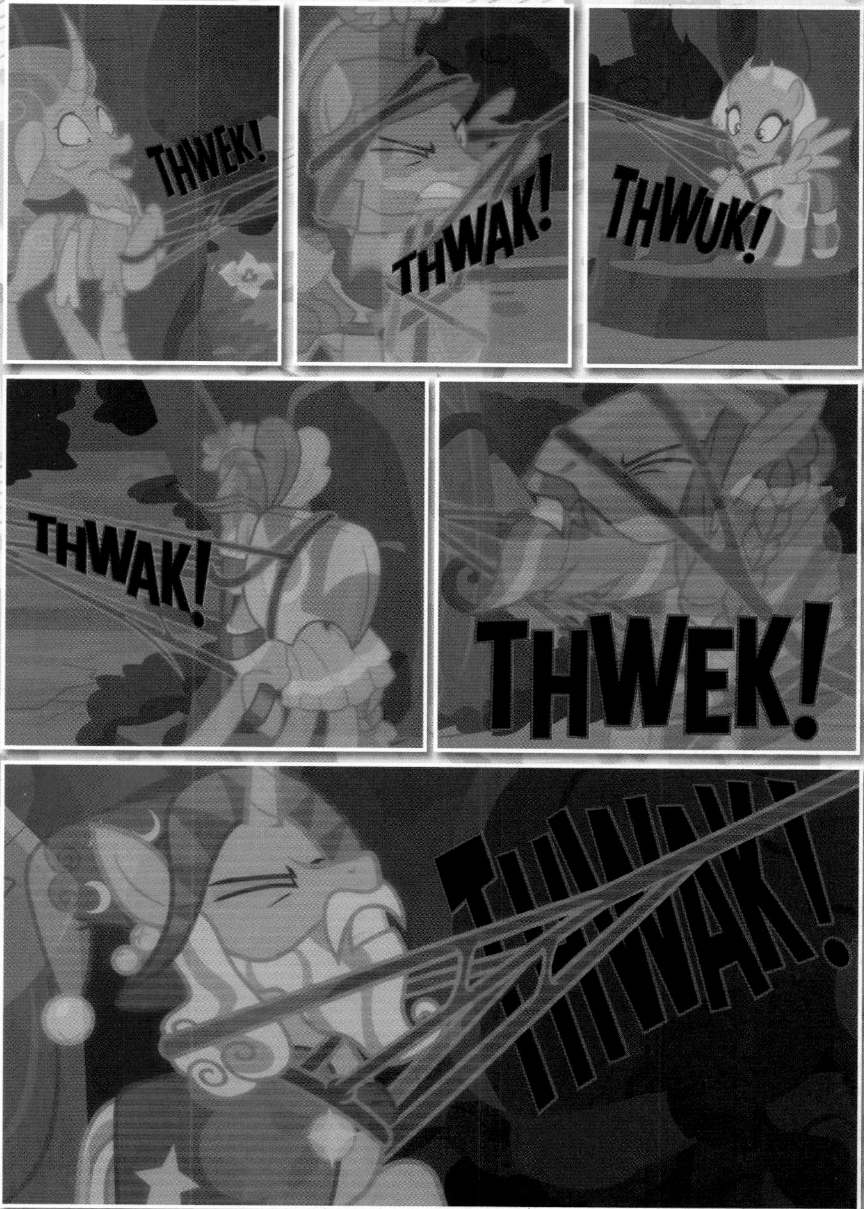
THWEK!
THWAK!
THWUK!
THWAK!
THWEK!
THWAK!

UMPF!

BWAH HA HA HA

DRAWING ME HERE WILL ONLY MAKE ME *STRONGER.*

YOU...

...WILL NEVER *DEFEAT* ME!

WE DID NOT
COME HERE TO
DEFEAT YOU...

ZxZxZxRRRRNNNN

SNAP!

ZxZxZxRRRRNNNN

THE OLD BOOK
RISES BEHIND
STARSWIRL...

...AND FIRES
A BOLT OF
MAGIC...

ZXORT

ZXIP!

ZXIP!

...FREEING THE PILLARS OF EQUESTRIA.

ZXIP!

ZXIP!

ZXIP!

AND SHINING LIGHT ON THE PONY OF SHADOWS.

WHAT ARE YOU DOING?!

WE CAME TO CONTAIN YOU.

ZXRRRRNNNNNGGGG

RAWRL!

VORT!!

UH—

WELL, YOU DID ASK FOR A MAGICAL EXPLANATION.

WHAT JUST HAPPENED?

IT LOOKED LIKE STARSWIRL CAST A SPELL THAT BANISHED THE PONY OF SHADOWS.

OF COURSE!

POWERFUL MAGIC LIKE THAT WOULD LEAVE AN IMPRESSION ON THIS PLACE.

BRINGING THE BOOK BACK HERE LET US SEE WHAT HAPPENED.

WHICH WAS WHAT?

STARSWIRL AND THE REST OF THE PILLARS...

...SACRIFICED THEMSELVES TO SAVE EQUESTRIA.

LATER AT THE CASTLE OF FRIENDSHIP...

IT'S AMAZING TO THINK ONE OF THE GREAT MYSTERIES OF EQUESTRIA...

...WAS SOLVED WITH A MUSTY OLD BOOK FROM AN ANTIQUE SHOP.

BUT I WOULDN'T SAY THE MYSTERY'S SOLVED.

STAR-SWIRL'S SPELL WAS ONE OF THE MOST POWERFUL FEATS OF MAGIC IN ALL OF HISTORY.

IT'LL TAKE *YEARS* OF STUDY BEFORE WE FULLY UNDERSTAND IT.

HHHRRRNNNNNN

SUNBURST OPENS THE DOOR TO TWILIGHT'S LIBRARY...

I THINK I UNDERSTAND THE SPELL!

SHORTLY...

I KNOW I'VE FINISHED ONE OF STARSWIRL'S SPELLS BEFORE...

...BUT THIS WAS ON A WHOLE DIFFERENT LEVEL!

ONCE STARLIGHT SET ME ON THE RIGHT TRACK WITH HIS CRAZY *HORNWRITING*...

...I WENT THROUGH THE JOURNAL AGAIN...

...AND IT'S AMAZING!

TWILIGHT, DARLING, WE UNDERSTAND YOU'RE EXCITED...

...BUT THAT'S ALL WE UNDERSTAND.

YEAH. WHAT EXACTLY IS SO AMAZING?

ONLY HOW STARSWIRL AND THE OTHER PILLARS SENT THE PONY OF SHADOWS TO LIMBO!

THEY DID *WHAT* NOW?

TWILIGHT REVEALS AN INTRICATE DIORAMA.

I THOUGHT YOU'D NEVER ASK.

THEY USED THEIR MAGIC TO OPEN A PORTAL BETWEEN WORLDS...

...TO LIMBO, AND PULLED THE PONY OF SHADOWS INSIDE.

STARSWIRL THOUGHT THE ONLY WAY TO TRAP THE PONY OF SHADOWS IN LIMBO...

...WAS FOR THE PILLARS TO TAKE HIM THERE.

SO THEY GOT STUCK TOO!

THE PONY OF SHADOWS MUST HAVE BEEN REALLY *AWFUL* FOR THEM TO DO THAT.

I SUPPOSE BEING TRAPPED FOR ALL TIME WITH A SUPER-DUPER BAD GUY IN LIMBO MIGHT BE OKAY...

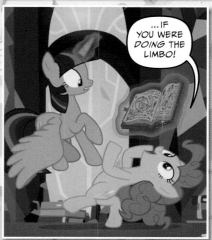

...IF YOU WERE *DOING* THE LIMBO!

BUT THAT'S STILL PUSHING IT.

THE THING IS...

...I THINK I CAN GET THEM OUT.

TWILIGHT, ARE YOU SERIOUS?

YOU CAN SAVE THE MOST LEGENDARY PONIES OF ALL TIME?

I DON'T KNOW.

OPENING PORTALS BETWEEN WORLDS DIDN'T WORK OUT WELL FOR ME.

ARE YOU SURE IT'S SAFE?

FIRST OF ALL, *YOU* OPENED PORTALS THROUGH TIME.

AND SECOND OF ALL, STARSWIRL WROTE THE SPELL YOU USED TO DO IT.

IF HE'D BEEN HERE, HE COULD HAVE STOPPED IT.

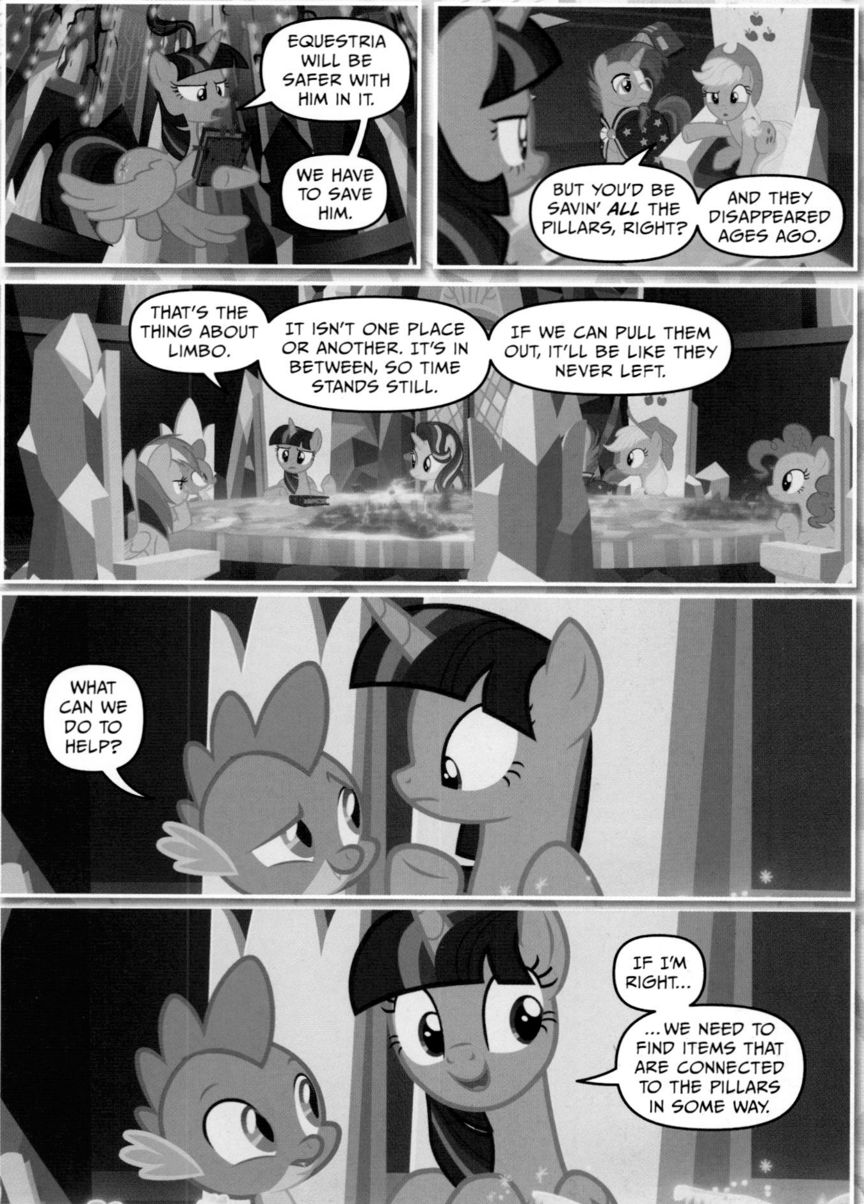
EQUESTRIA WILL BE SAFER WITH HIM IN IT.
WE HAVE TO SAVE HIM.
BUT YOU'D BE SAVIN' ALL THE PILLARS, RIGHT?
AND THEY DISAPPEARED AGES AGO.
THAT'S THE THING ABOUT LIMBO.
IT ISN'T ONE PLACE OR ANOTHER. IT'S IN BETWEEN, SO TIME STANDS STILL.
IF WE CAN PULL THEM OUT, IT'LL BE LIKE THEY NEVER LEFT.
WHAT CAN WE DO TO HELP?
IF I'M RIGHT...
...WE NEED TO FIND ITEMS THAT ARE CONNECTED TO THE PILLARS IN SOME WAY.

ARGH!

SLAM!

YOU MEAN, LIKE, STUFF THAT BELONGED TO THEM?

HOW WOULD WE KNOW WHAT TO LOOK FOR?

OR WHERE?

LUCKILY, STARSWIRL TOOK A *LOT* OF NOTES.

TWILIGHT FINDS HER PLACE AND BEGINS READING ALOUD...

"MY COMPATRIOTS ARE AS VARIED AS EQUESTRIA ITSELF AND HAIL FROM EVERY CORNER OF OUR LAND..."

"...BRINGING WITH THEM ARTIFACTS AND TALISMANS OF GREAT POWER..."

UM, TWILIGHT, WHAT ARE YOU DOING?

ZXZXZRRRRNNNN

GAH!

ZXZXZXRRRNNN

I'M NOT DOING ANYTHING!

ROCKHOOF'S SHOVEL!

THAT'S MAGNUS'S SHIELD!

MISTMANE'S FLOWER!

MEADOW-BROOK'S MASK!

AND THE BLINDFOLD SOMNAMBULA WORE...

...WHEN SHE FACED THAT NASTY SPHINX!

I GUESS WE DON'T NEED TO FIGURE OUT WHO SHOULD GET WHAT.

ROCKHOOF'S VILLAGE.

WHSK!
WHSK!

PROFESSOR! IT'S A MIGHTY HELM HEADPIECE!

MAYBE IT BELONGED TO ROCKHOOF HIMSELF!

THIS BELONGED TO A *REAL* PONY.

OH, I CAN GUARANTEE ROCKHOOF...

...WAS AS REAL AS YOU AND ME.

OH TEE-HEE!

AND I SUPPOSE THAT RAVINE WAS DUG WITH HIS *TRUSTY SHOVEL*...

...TO SAVE THE VILLAGE FROM AN *ERUPTING VOLCANO*.

PROBABLY.

I LOVE OLD LEGENDS AS MUCH AS ANYPONY...

...BUT A PONY STRONG ENOUGH TO SAVE A VILLAGE FROM RUSHING LAVA WITH A SHOVEL IS *PREPOSTEROUS!*

KRAK!

SMAK!

RUMMMBLE

FAH-RUP!

WHUMP

EEEEKK!

BLNK

HMPF!

OH.

HNNNNGH!

HEE-YUH!

WHOOOOSH

I CAN'T BELIEVE YOU JUST DID THAT. YOU SAVED US!

I BET IF YOU TOLD SOMEPONY ELSE THE STORY IT MIGHT SOUND...

...PREPOSTEROUS.

TAP TAP

WE'LL I'LL BE!

YOU'VE NEVER SEEN THAT BEFORE?

APPLEJACK ENTERS THE HIDDEN CHAMBER...

CHOMP!

I SUPPOSE SOME STORIES *MIGHT* BE TRUE...

ZZZZZZRRRNNNNN

...AND ROCKHOOF'S APPEARS TO BE ONE OF THEM.

AT THE BOTANICAL GARDENS...

VVVRRRRRNNNNNN

RUSTLE

THERE IT IS!

ZXZXZXIRRRNNNNN

WHAP!

OUCH!

YOU KEEP THOSE HOOFS TO YOURSELF, DEARIE!

THIS PLACE HAS BEEN IN MY FAMILY FOR GENERATIONS...

...AND I'M NOT ABOUT TO LET SOME *WHIPPER-SNAPPER*...

TIME WAS, PONIES CAME FROM FAR AND WIDE TO SEE THESE GARDENS.

BUT THAT FLOWER'S THE ONLY WORTH-WHILE THING LEFT.

THAT GIVES ME AN IDEA...

RARITY USES HER MAGIC...

VVVRRRRRNNNNNN

VROOOOSH

...AND STARTS TENDING TO THE GARDEN...

VVVVRRRRRNNNNN

I... I CAN'T...

SNIP!

WHAT DID YOU DO?!

PERHAPS IT JUST SEEMED LIKE YOUR GARDENS WERE WORTH-LESS...

...BUT A LITTLE PRUNING...

...CAN WORK WONDERS.

OF COURSE YOU'LL HAVE TO LOOK AFTER MORE THAN JUST ONE FLOWER NOW.

YOU'VE GIVEN ME BACK MY FAMILY'S LEGACY.

THE FLOWER YOU WANTED SEEMS LIKE A FAIR TRADE FOR THAT.

IZIZIZRRRNNNN

IN THE DRAGONLANDS...

POOF!

I CAN'T BELIEVE FLASH MAGNUS'S SHEILD ENDED UP IN THE DRAGONLANDS.

GOOD THING YOU BROUGHT THE...

...OFFICIAL EQUESTRIAN FRIENDSHIP AMBASSADOR TO THE DRAGONS...

...TO HELP YOU NAVIGATE OUR CUSTOMS.

LIKE OUR FAVORITE SPORT—

GORGE SURFING!

WA-HOO!

YEAH!

SPLURSH!

SKKRRRRTT

HOORAH!

HA-HA HA!

OKAY. THAT WAS AWESOME.

DRAGON LORD EMBER COMMANDED US TO MAKE PEACE WITH PONIES...

...BUT THAT DOESN'T MEAN YOU CAN SURF IN OUR SPOT.

I—

WHOA! FELLAS.

AS THE OFFICIAL EQUESTRIAN FRIENDSHIP AMBASSADOR TO THE DRAGONS...

...I HAVE TO SAY, THAT'S NOT VERY FRIENDLY.

WHAT DO YOU KNOW?!

THE PUNY PONY DRAGON'S STICKING UP FOR HIS PONY PAL.

WHUMP

HEY!

THAT'S AN ANCIENT PONY ARTIFACT.

HOOVES OFF MY GORGE BOARD!

THWAT!

I *FOUND* IT IN THE DESERT AND *FINDERS KEEPERS*.

IT ISN'T YOURS.

IT SURE LOOKS LIKE MINE.

BUT, I MIGHT CONSIDER RACING YOU FOR IT.

NO PROBLEM.

UM, NO.

I MEAN YOU.

YEAH, HA-HA.

UH...?

WHOOOOSH

HEY, SPIKE!

SPPLRPTFFFFFT!

ON YOUR MARKS!

GET SET!

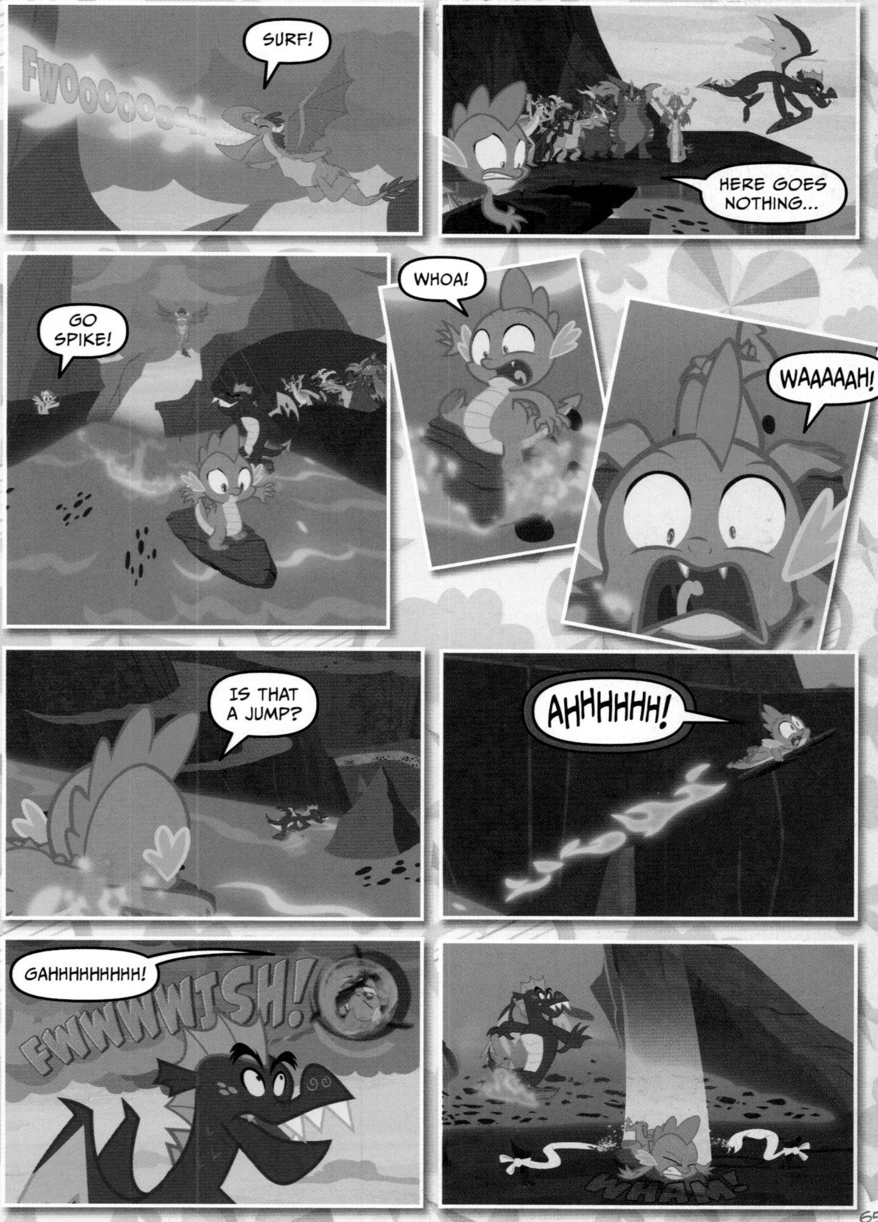
SURF!
FWOOOOOOSH
HERE GOES NOTHING...
GO SPIKE!
WHOA!
WAAAAAH!
IS THAT A JUMP?
AHHHHHH!
GAHHHHHHHHH!
FWWWWISH!
WHAM!

WAIT... HUH?!

I WON?

GIVE UP THE SHIELD, GARBLE.

I WON!

GARBLE PUTS THE SHIELD ON HIS BACK.

LORD EMBER ONLY COMMANDED US TO BE NICE TO PONIES.

SHE NEVER SAID ANYTHING ABOUT *PONY-LOVING* DRAGONS.

SINCE DRAGON LORD EMBER COMMANDED YOU TO MAKE PEACE WITH PONIES...

...YOU CAN'T VERY WELL ATTACK ONE OF THEIR FRIENDS, CAN YOU?

I GUESS WE'LL FIND OUT!

HRMP!

CHUK!

FWHIP!

GAH!

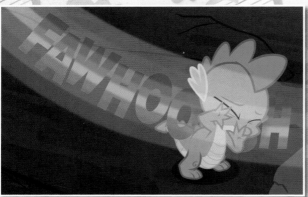

BLINK!

HEY, GARBLE, I THINK YOU LOST YOUR ROCK.

DON'T *WORRY*, I'LL GIVE IT *BACK*!

ARGH!

SLAMMM

SPIKE, ARE YOU ALL—

SQUEEEEZE

WHY IS HE ALWAYS HIDING BEHIND PONIES?

I WASN'T HIDING WHEN I BEAT YOU DOWN THE RIDGE.

YOU FELL!

WOW, YOU MUST BE SLOW...

...IF ALL SPIKE HAD TO DO TO WIN WAS FALL DOWN.

I'M FASTER THAN YOU!

DOUBT IT.

FINE. I'LL RACE YOU BACK TO THE TOP.

IF YOU WIN, YOU CAN HAVE YOUR PONY JUNK.

BUT IF I WIN, YOU'LL LEAVE, AND I GET TO *GIVE IT* TO HIM!

I'M PRETTY SURE I COULD BEAT YOU ANYWAY...

...BUT WITH THAT HEAVY HUNK OF METAL ON YOUR BACK, IT'LL BE A SNAP.

OH YEAH, THANKS FOR THE TIP.

THUD

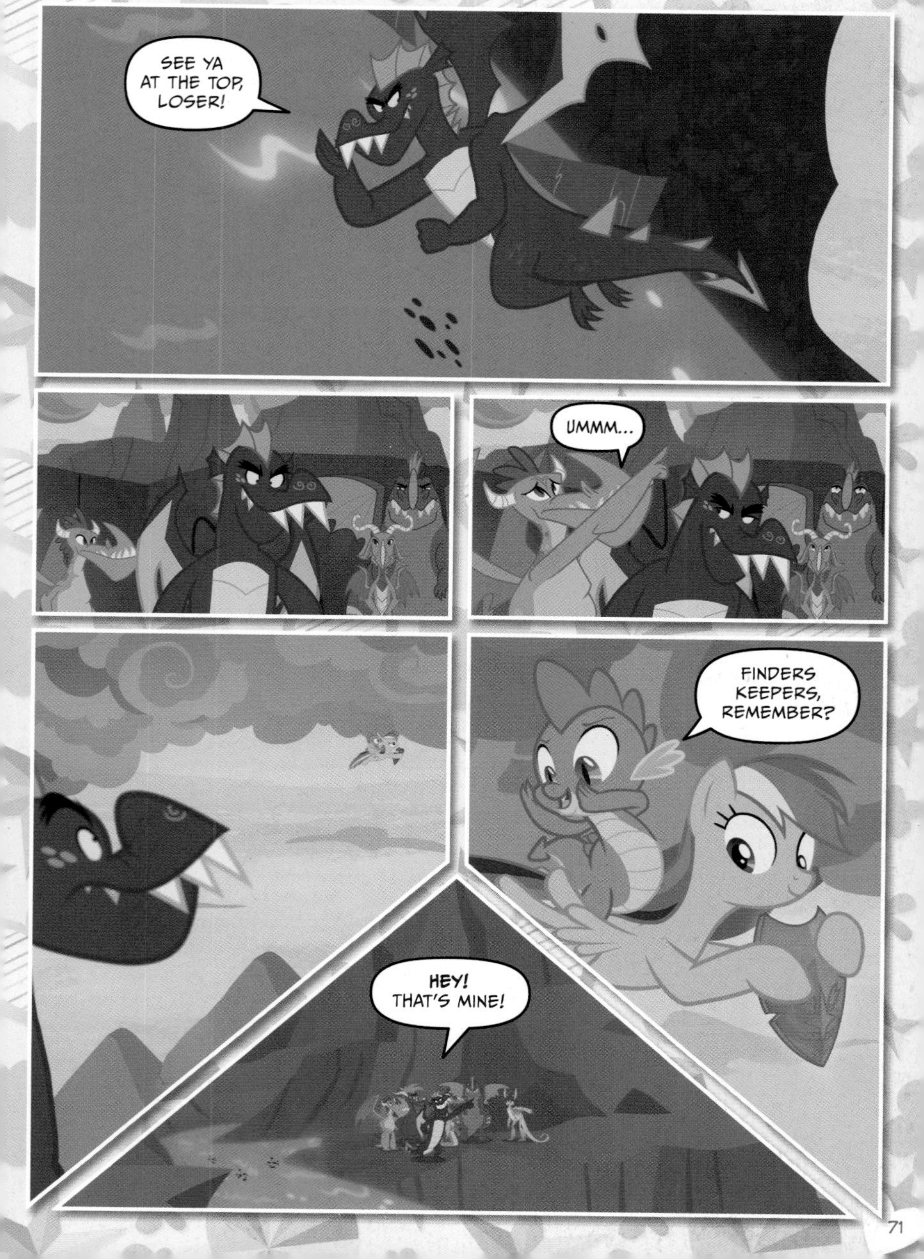
SEE YA AT THE TOP, LOSER!
UMMM...
FINDERS KEEPERS, REMEMBER?
HEY! THAT'S MINE!

HAYSEED SWAMP.

BBZZZZZZZZZ

THERE THEY ARE.

RUSTLE

HEY, BEES! OVER HERE!

BBZZZZZZZZZ

FOLLOW ME!

BBZZZZZZZZZ

JUST REMEMBER NOT TO TURN AWAY FROM THEM, CATTAIL.

FLASH BEES CAN GET PRETTY AGGRESSIVE...

YOU KNOW, YOU DIDN'T HAVE TO HELP WITH THIS.

I'D HAVE LENT YOU THE MASK ANYWAY.

I KNOW...

...BUT I COULDN'T LEAVE WITHOUT HELPING.

OHHHH!

ZXZXZXZRRRNNNNNN

WAHHHHHHH?!

NEAR SOMNAMBULA.

IT'S *GROSS!*

I DON'T THINK *ANYPONY* CAN FIND ANYTHING IN THERE.

I WOULDN'T GIVE UP HOPE JUST YET.

PINKIE, CAN YOU SEE ANYTHING?!

POP!

GURRRGGGLL

THIS OLD BLINDFOLD WAS STUCK IN THE DRAIN.

WEREN'T YOU LOOKING FOR A BLINDFOLD?

OH, YEAH!

WOOSH!

BZZZZWZZRRRLLLMMM

AT PONEHENGE...

I CAN'T BELIEVE I'M GOING TO MEET STARSWIRL THE BEARDED!

YOU KNOW, OUTSIDE OF MY DREAMS.

I CAN'T BELIEVE YOU'RE ACTUALLY GOING THROUGH WITH IT.

WHAT DO YOU MEAN?

I'M ALL FOR PUSHING THE ENVELOPE, OBVIOUSLY...

...BUT THIS IS PRETTY *OUT THERE* FOR YOU, TWILIGHT.

WHAT'S *OUT THERE* ABOUT SAVING *THE MOST LEGENDARY PONIES OF ALL TIME* FROM A THOUSAND-YEAR-OLD PRISON?

WELL, NOTHING, WHEN YOU SAY IT LIKE THAT.

UNLESS... *THE MOST LEGENDARY PONIES OF ALL TIME KNEW WHAT THEY WERE DOING...*

...AND WE SHOULDN'T MESS WITH IT.

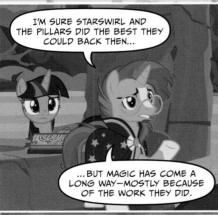

I'M SURE STARSWIRL AND THE PILLARS DID THE BEST THEY COULD BACK THEN...

...BUT MAGIC HAS COME A LONG WAY—MOSTLY BECAUSE OF THE WORK THEY DID.

THAT'S TRUE.

AND YOU DID GET YOUR WINGS...

...FROM FINISHING ONE OF STARSWIRL'S SPELLS...

EXACTLY.

BUT THEN I MESSED WITH ONE AND NEARLY DESTROYED THE UNIVERSE, SO...

STARLIGHT, STARSWIRL THE BEARDED IS THE *GREATEST WIZARD* WHO EVER LIVED.

THE CHANCE TO HAVE HIM BACK IN EQUESTRIA IS WORTH THE RISK.

THAT'S GOOD NEWS!

THUNK!

OTHERWISE, WE'D HAVE BROUGHT THIS SHIELD FOR NOTHING!

I HOPE YOU DON'T THINK YOU'RE THE ONLY ONE TO FIND YOUR ARTIFACT...

...BECAUSE THIS HERE SHOVEL SAYS OTHERWISE.

HONESTLY, YOU TWO. *NOT EVERYTHING IS A COMPETITION.*

THOUGH MISTMANE'S FLOWER IS BY FAR THE MOST ATTRACTIVE OF THE ARTIFACTS.

YOU'RE JUST SAYING THAT BECAUSE YOU DIDN'T HAVE TO...

...SCUBA DIVE IN A PIT OF GREEN SLIME TO GET YOURS.

OR MOVE A FLASH BEE HIVE.

GOOD WORK EVERYONE.

LET'S DO THIS!

UGH.

VORL!

ZORT!

ALL THEIR MAGIC FOCUSES ON THE BOOK!

WHICH RELEASES ITS OWN BEAM OF MAGIC!

THAT RADIATES ACROSS PONEHENGE!

IT'S WORKING!

I CAN'T BELIEVE IT!

UM, GUYS?

WHAT'S HAPPENING?

VIP!

THERE, HANGING IN MID-AIR...

IT'S THE PILLARS!

SLAMM!

WHAM!

WHUMP!

WHAT... WHAT HAS HAPPENED?

IT WORKED! WE BROUGHT YOU BACK!

TO WHERE?

YOU AND THE OTHERS HAVE BEEN TRAPPED IN LIMBO FOR A THOUSAND YEARS... **...BUT I FIGURED OUT HOW TO GET YOU HOME.**

WHAT?!

NO, NO, NO, NO, YOU MUST UNDO WHAT YOU'VE DONE!

BUT WHY?

I MEAN, I DON'T THINK I CAN.

YOU CANNOT BRING US BACK—

BUT I DID.

I BROUGHT ALL THE PILLARS BACK.

YOU CANNOT BRING *ONLY* THE PILLARS BACK...

KRA-KOOOM!

NO!

KA-ROOOOSH

BWAH HA HA HA

OH NO!

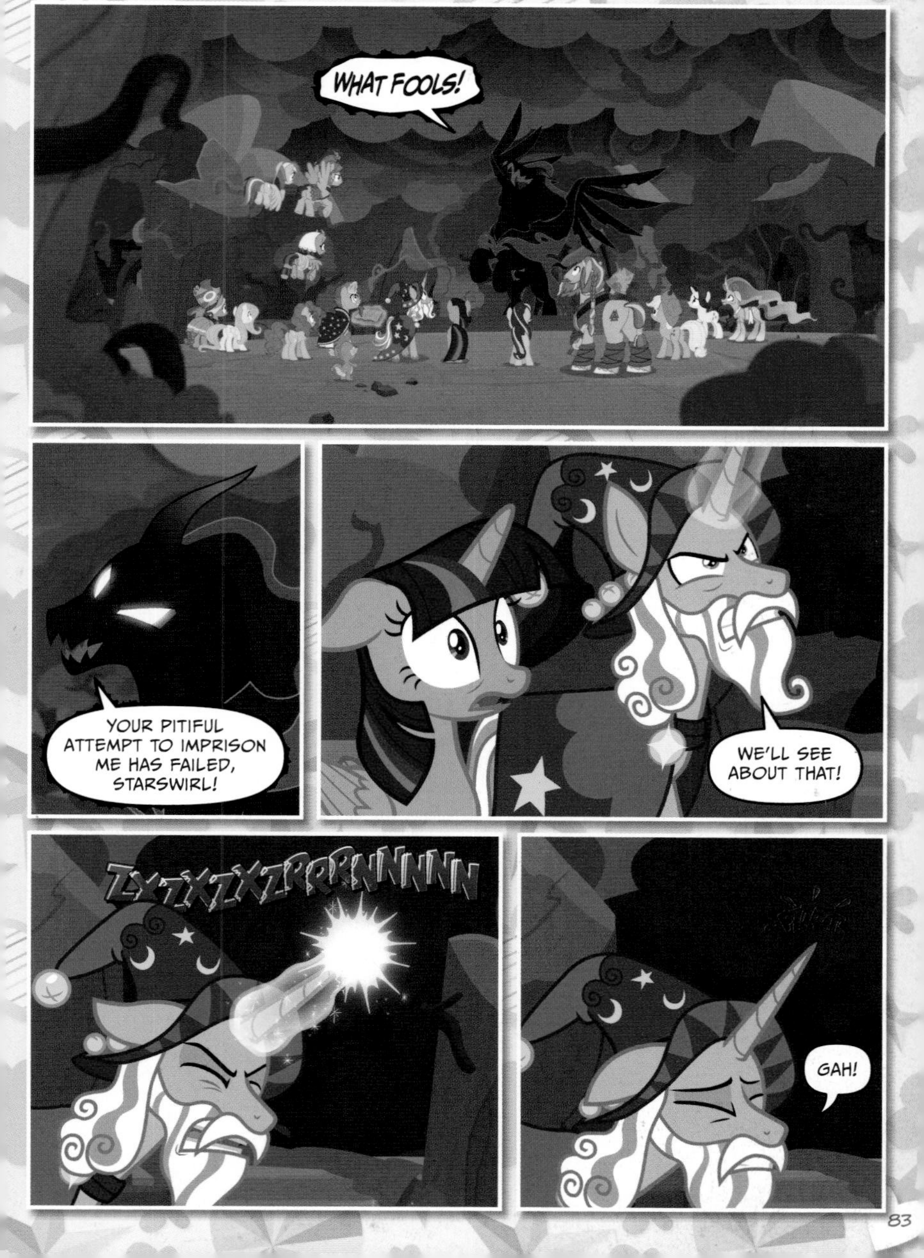
WHAT FOOLS!
YOUR PITIFUL ATTEMPT TO IMPRISON ME HAS FAILED, STARSWIRL!
WE'LL SEE ABOUT THAT!
ZYZIXZIXZRRRNNNNNN
GAH!

YOU MUST RETURN US TO LIMBO.

IT'S THE ONLY WAY TO STOP HIM.

BUT I ONLY FIGURED OUT HOW TO BRING YOU BACK.

WORKING ON IT... NO TABLE OF CONTENTS...

ALLOW ME TO ASSIST.

FWHOO

FWIPPP

THWAK!

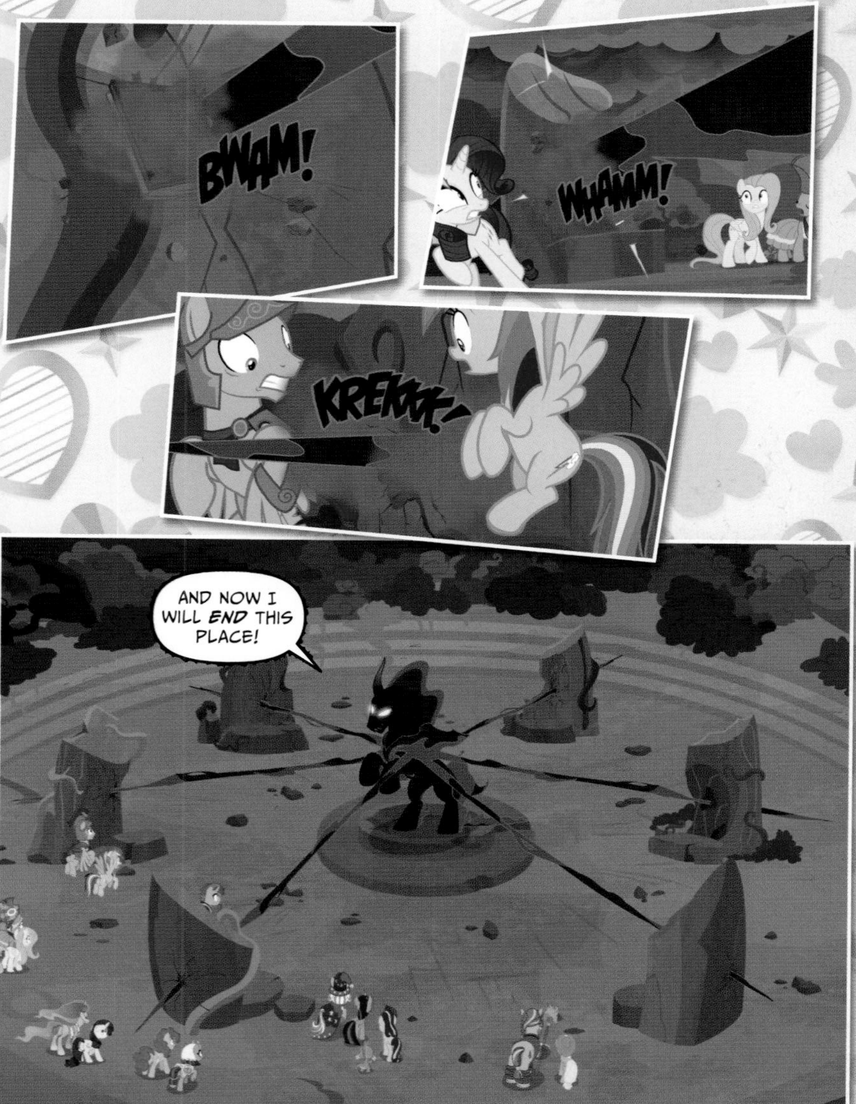
BWAM!
WHAMM!
KREKKK!
AND NOW I WILL *END* THIS PLACE!

NO!

WITHOUT THE POWER OF *PONEHENGE*, YOUR BANISHING SPELL IS USELESS.

YOU HAVE STUDIED MY WRITINGS.

SURELY YOU HAVE SOME *OTHER* PLAN.

NO. I JUST WANTED TO SAVE YOU, I DIDN'T THINK—

DON'T FRET.

WHEN I EXTINGUISH THE LIGHT AND HOPE OF THIS MISERABLE WORLD...

YOU WON'T REMEMBER *ANY* OF THIS.

ZORT!

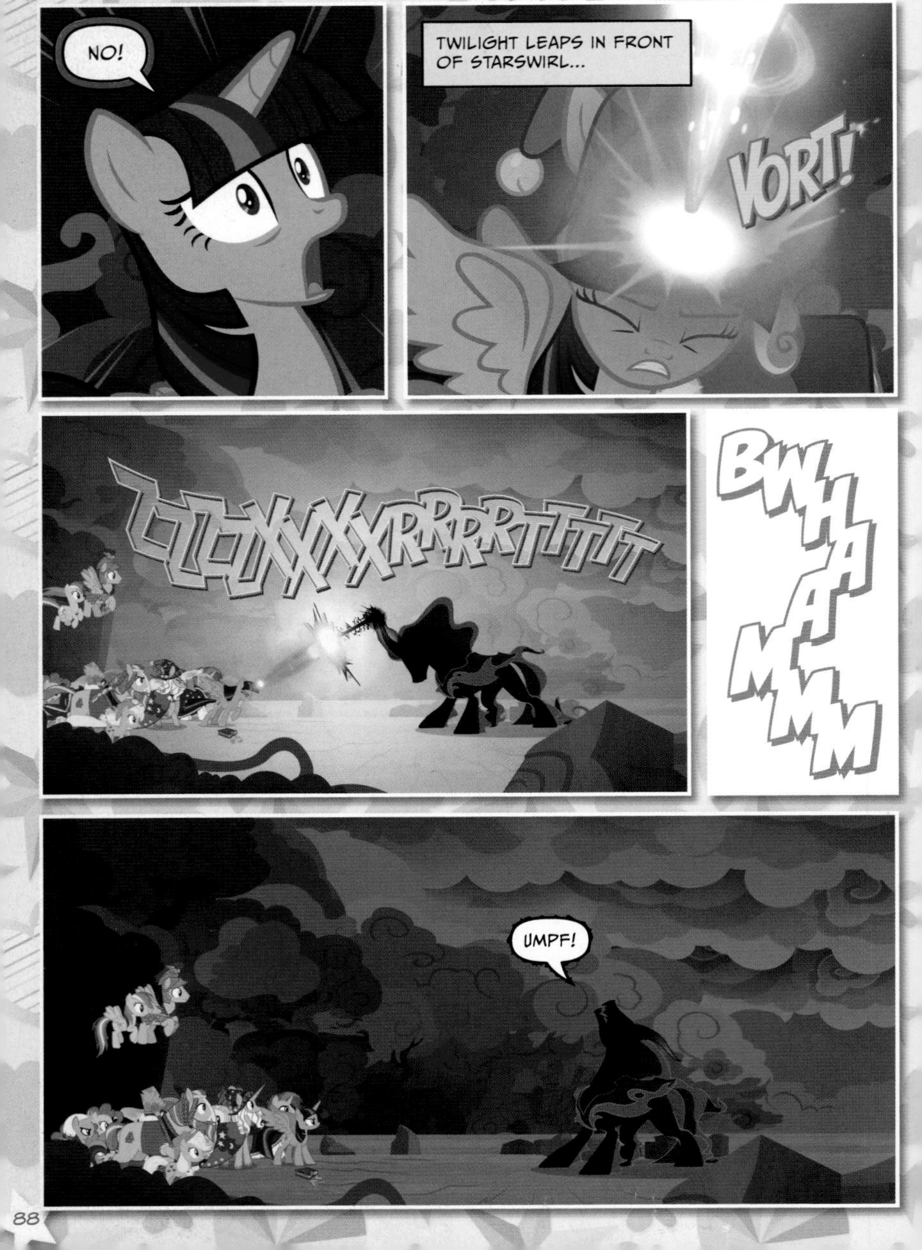
NO!
TWILIGHT LEAPS IN FRONT OF STARSWIRL...
VORT!
BWHAAMMM
UMPF!

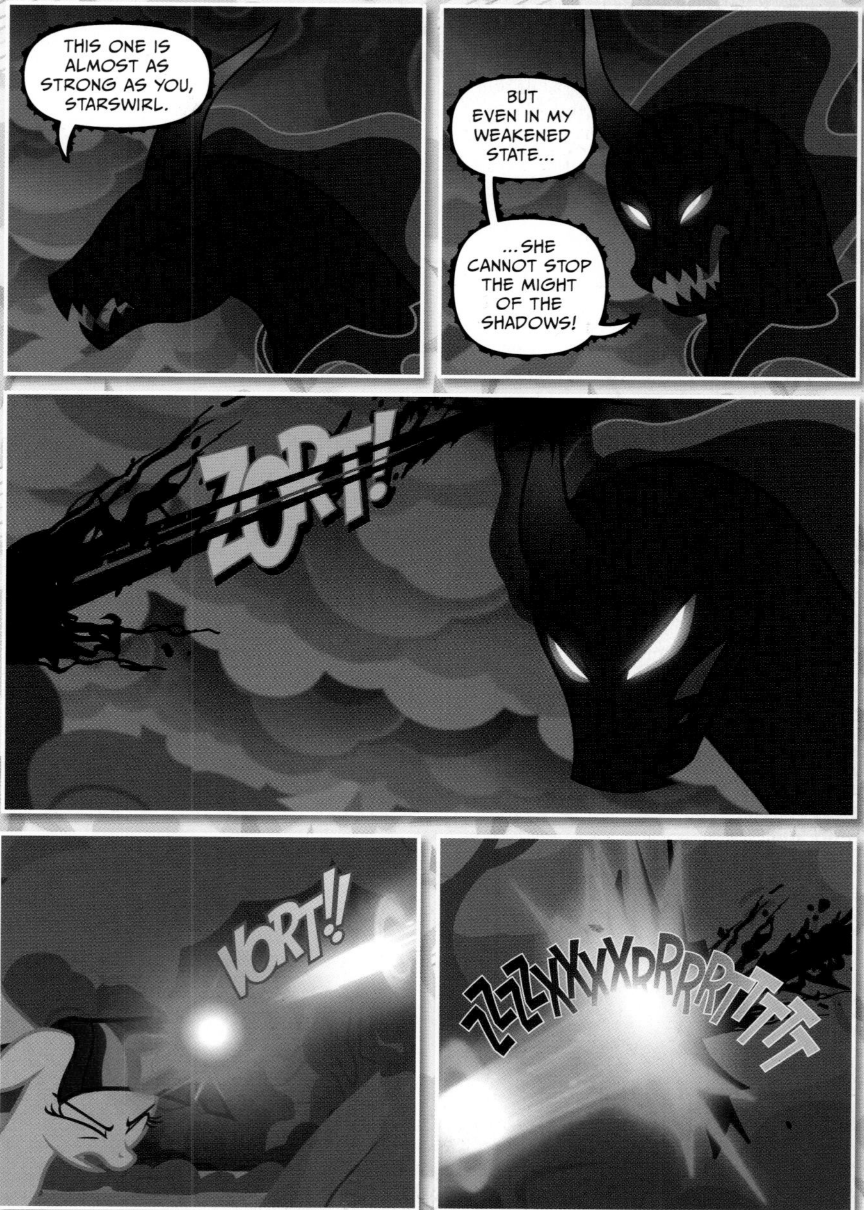
THIS ONE IS ALMOST AS STRONG AS YOU, STARSWIRL.
BUT EVEN IN MY WEAKENED STATE...
...SHE CANNOT STOP THE MIGHT OF THE SHADOWS!
ZORT!
VORT!!
ZZZZXXXXRRRRTTTTT

GAH!

VIPP!

LUCKY FOR HER, SHE'S NOT ALONE.

ZZZXXXRRRTTTTT

ZZZXXXRRRTTTTT

ARRRGGGHHH!

KNOW THIS, FIEND. WE WILL NOT REST...

...UNTIL WE FIND A WAY TO RETURN YOU TO LIMBO.

NEVER. YOUR DAYS OF GLORY ARE THROUGH, STARSWIRL.

NOW MY DARK POWER WILL REIGN, AND YOU WILL BOW TO ME!

FLUMP

WHOOOSH

KRZXXT KRZXX

UM... WHERE'D HE GO?

THAT IS A RIDDLE WE MUST UNRAVEL, AND QUICKLY.

HOW LONG HAVE WE BEEN GONE?

OVER A THOUSAND YEARS.

GAH!

HUH?!

THEN MY SPELL WORKED...

...BEFORE IT WAS MEDDLED WITH.

AND THE REALM HAS BEEN AT PEACE FOR A MILLENNIUM.

WELL... WE DID HAVE TO SAVE EVERYPONY FROM *NIGHTMARE MOON*...

...AND *DISCORD*, AND *CHRYSALIS*...

...AND *KING SOMBRA*...

...AND *LORD TIREK*.

AND THERE WAS THAT ONE TIME WHEN *STARLIGHT* TRAVELED THROUGH TIME...

...AND ALMOST DESTROYED LIFE AS WE KNOW IT!

HI.

BUT THAT'S ALL IN THE PAST.

IF YOU ARE TRULY THIS ACCOMPLISHED...

...WE WILL STOP THE PONY OF SHADOWS TWICE AS FAST TOGETHER.

WE SHALL SEE. IT IS AN EASY THING TO *SAY* YOU HAVE SAVED THE WORLD.

IT IS QUITE ANOTHER TO DO IT.

OH, WE'VE SAVED THE WORLD, BEARDO.

AND WE CAN DO IT AGAIN.

BE THAT AS IT MAY, MY SPUNKY COMPANION...

TAP!

THE PROBLEM OF LOCATING THE PONY OF SHADOWS REMAINS.

AND THIS LAND IS VAST.

IT SOUNDS LIKE YOU NEED A MAP!

"LUCKILY, WE HAVE JUST THE THING."

SOMETHING ABOUT THIS MAGIC SEEMS FAMILIAR...

ZZYZXRRNNNN

96

VIP!

FWISH!

ZX-ZXRRRRNNNN

WOW!

WHOA!

DID YOU KNOW HE COULD DO THAT?

HE'S STARSWIRL.

HE CAN DO ANYTHING!

THIS MAP AND, INDEED, THIS VERY CASTLE HAVE *GROWN* FROM THE SEED WE PLANTED...

...A THOUSAND YEARS AGO.

THEN IT DID WORK!

THEN *WHAT* WORKED?!

EACH OF US INFUSED A CRYSTAL SEED WITH OUR MAGIC...

...IN HOPES THAT IT WOULD GROW INTO A FORCE FOR GOOD.

WE WANTED TO LEAVE SOMETHING TO PROTECT THE REALM IN OUR ABSENCE.

BUT WE NEVER DREAMED OUR GIFT WOULD BECOME SO POWERFUL.

HOLD UP. Y'ALL MEAN THE ELEMENTS CAME FROM YOU?

HMMM...

YOU KNOW, THE SPARKLY CRYSTAL THINGS... ...THAT GROW FROM THE TREE OF HARMONY... ...AND REPRESENT EACH OF US?

LAUGHTER!

HONESTY!

GENEROSITY.

LOYALTY.

KINDNESS.

AND *magic!*

THE REFLECTIONS OF OUR OWN ELEMENTS OF HOPE...

STRENGTH.

BEAUTY.

BRAVERY.

HEALING.

AND SORCERY.

WE HAD NO IDEA OUR SMALL SEED...

...WOULD BLOOM INTO THE LIVING SPIRIT OF THE LAND.

I AM GLAD OUR MANTLES HAVE PASSED TO SUCH CAPABLE PONIES.

MORE IMPORTANTLY, WE NO LONGER NEED PONEHENGE TO SEND OUR FOE BACK TO LIMBO.

WE CAN USE THE STORED MAGIC IN THIS TREE OF HARMONY.

BUT DOESN'T A BANISHING SPELL TAKE A LOT OF POWER?

WE'D HAVE TO SACRIFICE THE ELEMENTS FOR THAT.

YES, THAT IS CORRECT.

THEY'LL BE GONE... FOREVER?

STARSWIRL, I DON'T THINK THE TREE CAN SURVIVE WITHOUT THE ELEMENTS.

IF IT DIES, EQUESTRIA WILL SUFFER.

IF THE PONY OF SHADOWS HAS HIS WAY, YOUR LAND WILL NOT *EXIST*.

SO UNLESS YOU HAVE A BETTER IDEA...?

NO.

OUR FOE WILL SEEK DARK PLACES FROM WHICH TO DRAW POWER.

I WILL PREPARE MY SPELL...

...SO THAT WE MAY STRIKE AS SOON AS YOU FIND HIM.

WHAT ARE WE WAITING FOR?!

I LIKE YOUR SPIRIT!

YES!

YAY!

YEE!

OH NO.

LATER, IN TWILIGHT'S LIBRARY...

SEA PONY ETIQUETTE ISN'T GOING TO HELP RIGHT NOW, SPIKE.

UHHH... TWILIGHT?

WHAT ABOUT THIS ONE?

ARE YOU OKAY?

I JUST UNLEASHED ULTIMATE EVIL...

...AND *DOOMED* EQUESTRIA BECAUSE I WAS OBSESSED WITH MEETING MY *IDOL*.

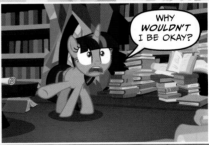

WHY *WOULDN'T* I BE OKAY?

WHAAM

PFFFT

YOU DIDN'T KNOW THAT WOULD HAPPEN.

NOW THE *ELEMENTS OF HARMONY* WILL BE LOST TO FIX MY MISTAKE!

MAYBE THERE'S ANOTHER WAY...

IF THERE IS, TWILIGHT WILL FIND IT.

WWWRDNNNNN

YES!

IF THE PILLARS CAN HOLD OPEN THE GATEWAY TO LIMBO...

...A POWERFUL PONY CAN DO THE BANISHING SPELL HERSELF!

DO YOU *KNOW* WHAT THIS *MEANS?*

WHAAM

I CAN STOP CARRYING BOOKS?

THE PILLARS DON'T HAVE TO LEAVE EQUESTRIA!

EVEN THOUGH WE'LL LOSE THE ELEMENTS...

...WE'LL HAVE THE PONIES THAT CREATED THEM.

AND THE PONY OF SHADOWS WILL BE BANISHED FOR GOOD!

THAT'S GREAT...

...BUT I WAS THINKING OF ANOTHER WAY THAT MAYBE DOESN'T INVOLVE BANISHING...

...AT ALL?

STARSWIRL KNEW WHAT HE WAS DOING WHEN HE CAST THAT SPELL.

IF I CAN MAKE IT EVEN BETTER...

...MAYBE HE'LL SEE I TAKE MAGIC AS SERIOUSLY AS HE DOES.

VVVVRRNNNNN

STARLIGHT HAS A BAD FEELING...

108

HHHRRRRNNNNNN

HHHRRRNN

HHHRRRNN

IT SEEMS THE DARK PLACES STARSWIRL INDICATED ON THE MAP HAVE CHANGED.

CLOP   CLOP   CLOPPP

I BET THE PONY OF SHADOWS WOULD'VE LOVED THE GHASTLY CAVERNS...

...BEFORE A THOUSAND YEARS OF EROSION TURNED IT INTO THE GHASTLY GORGE.

THE APPELOOSIAN WASTES SURE SOUNDED DARK AND DESOLATE.

WHO KNEW THEY WOULD BECOME SUCH A POPULAR SQUARE DANCING DESTINATION?

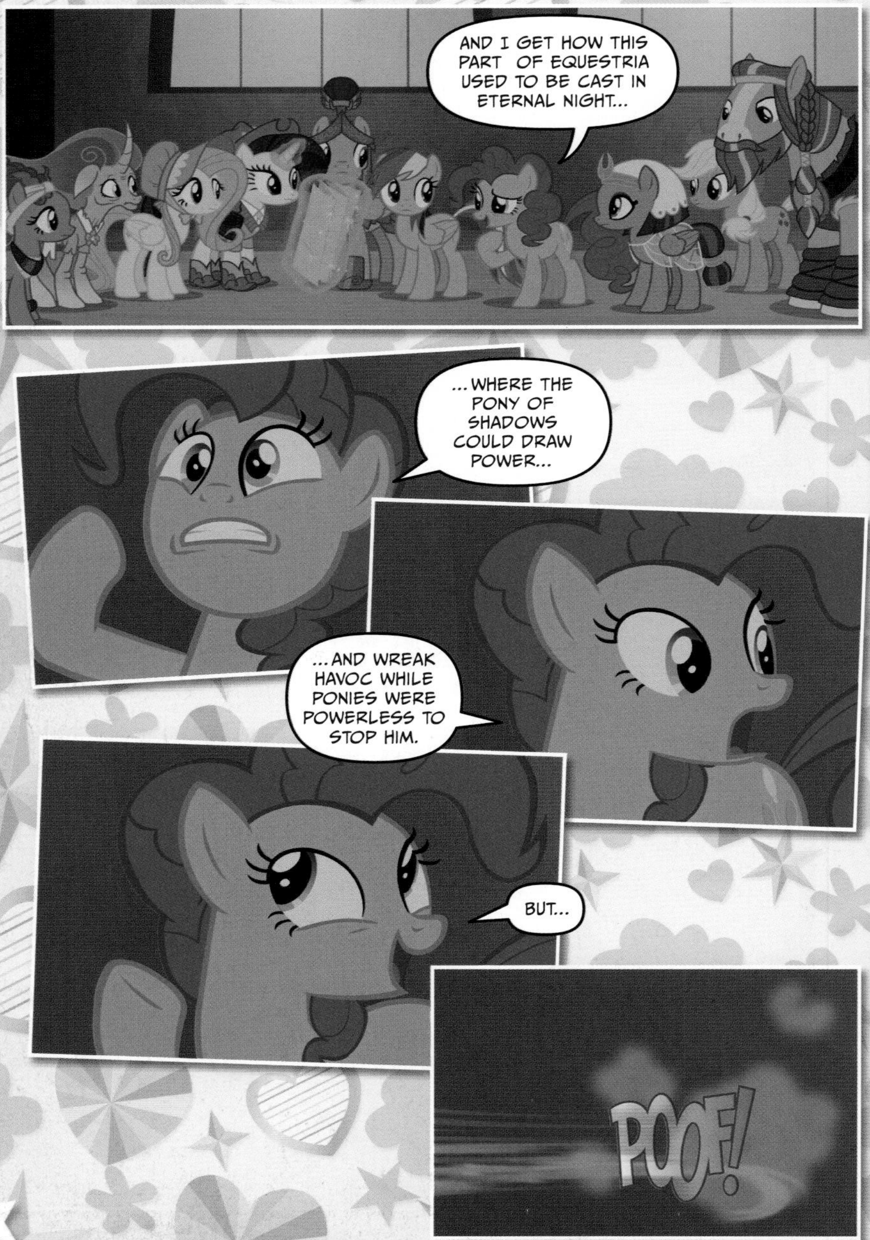
AND I GET HOW THIS PART OF EQUESTRIA USED TO BE CAST IN ETERNAL NIGHT...
...WHERE THE PONY OF SHADOWS COULD DRAW POWER...
...AND WREAK HAVOC WHILE PONIES WERE POWERLESS TO STOP HIM.
BUT...
POOF!

IT'S KINDA MADE A COMEBACK.

DID I MENTION IT'S REALLY BRIGHT?

SHE HAS A POINT.

WE CAN MARK THIS ONE OFF.

CHK-CHK

HMMMM...

IT SEEMS THERE ARE FEWER DARK CORNERS IN THE REALM THESE DAYS.

ZWAZRRWNNN

ISN'T THAT A GOOD THING?

TRUE. THE PONY OF SHADOWS WILL HAVE A HARD TIME REGAINING POWER.

WHEN HE REARS HIS HEAD, WE'LL BE READY!

CLUNK!

ISN'T THERE SOME WAY TO BANISH HIM WITHOUT LOSING ALL OF YOU?

I WISH THERE WERE.

BUT TO SAVE OUR HOME...

...WE ARE WILLING TO *LEAVE* IT.

I DON'T THINK YOU'LL HAVE TO!

BHWAAM

MY SPELL ISN'T FINISHED YET...

...BUT I THINK WE CAN SEND THE PONY OF SHADOWS TO LIMBO...

...WITHOUT ALL OF YOU HAVING TO GO AS WELL!

TWILIGHT PROUDLY PRESENTS THE SPELL TO STARSWIRL.

ZXZXZXZXZRRRNNNNNN

WHILE I *APPRECIATE* YOUR ENTHUSIASM, TWILIGHT...

KRRIIIPP

...THIS IS HARDLY THE TIME TO TAKE RISKS ON *HALF-BAKED* SPELLS.

HMPF.

BEGGING YOUR PARDON, *MR. THE BEARDED.*

BUT TWILIGHT DOESN'T DO ANYTHING *HALF-WAY.*

FWHIPP

ESPECIALLY NOT MAGIC!

SERIOUSLY! SHE GOT HER WINGS...

...BY FINISHING ONE OF *YOUR* SPELLS.

HER WORK IS CERTAINLY WORTH *READING...*

...BEFORE YOU *DISMISS* IT OUT OF *HOOF!*

UH-*HUH.*

WHILE IT IS AN *UNCONVENTIONAL* APPROACH...

...I BELIEVE IT COULD WORK.

HM. I SUPPOSE THERE IS A CHANCE...

BUT WE STILL HAVE NO IDEA WHERE TO FIND THE VILLAIN.

VVVUVRRRNNNNN

EVERYPONY'S CUTIE MARK STARTS TO GLOW!

VVVVURRRNNNNN

THEN GROUP TOGETHER ON THE CUTIE MAP!

MAYBE WE SHOULD TRY THERE.

VVVVURRRNNNNN

WHOA.

THE HOLLOW SHADES.

I THINK A BRANCH OF THE APPLE FAMILY LIVES THERE.

THEY'D HAVE TO BE PRETTY DISTANT.

THE *HOLLOW SHADES* WAS ABANDONED EONS AGO.

THAT'S ODD.

THE ONLY TIME THE MAP'S CALLED ALL OF US TO ONE PLACE WAS STARLIGHT'S VILLAGE.

SO IT'S LIKE A SUPER-VILLAIN TRACKER!

BWNK

NO OFFENSE.

DO YOU THINK THE MAP COULD BE TRYING TO TELL US WHERE THE PONY OF SHADOWS IS?

THE TREE OF HARMONY ACTING TO PROTECT THE LIGHT OF THE REALM...

I WILL MAKE MY NOTES ON THIS SPELL.

READY YOURSELVES FOR BATTLE.

UH...

I KNOW I'M NOT AS EXPERIENCED AS ALL OF YOU...

...BUT IS *BANISHMENT* REALLY THE *ONLY* OPTION?

I MEAN, IT'S BEEN A *LONG TIME.*

MAYBE THE PONY OF SHADOWS IS *READY TO TALK.*

I *DOUBT* WE CAN SAVE OUR HOMELAND WITH A *CONVERSATION.*

BUT WE COULD TRY.

STARLIGHT, I'M SURE STARSWIRL AND THE OTHERS *DID* TRY—A THOUSAND YEARS AGO.

THE PONY OF SHADOWS WAS NOT INTERESTED IN *RECONCILIATION*.

ONCE A *VILLAIN*, ALWAYS A *VILLAIN*.

TWILIGHT, SUNBURST, WOULD YOU ACCOMPANY ME?

I WISH TO REFINE THE SPELL FOR OUR USE.

COME! WE MUST PREPARE FOR THE STRUGGLE AHEAD.

I KNOW STARSWIRL IS A *GREAT* WIZARD...

...BUT THIS WHOLE PLAN SEEMS *WRONG*.

THE MAP'S ONLY EVER SENT US TO SOLVE FRIENDSHIP PROBLEMS.

MAYBE SO...

...BUT THE PONY OF SHADOWS DOESN'T REALLY SEEM LIKE THE FRIENDSHIP TYPE.

HONESTLY, WE DON'T KNOW ANYTHING ABOUT HIM.

NOPONY DOES.

THAT'S NOT ENTIRELY TRUE.

A FEW MOMENTS LATER...

YOU ALL KNEW THE PONY OF SHADOWS BEFORE HE BECAME WHAT HE IS NOW.

YOU MUST HAVE BEEN FRIENDS, SO WHAT HAPPENED?

THE TALE OF OUR RIFT IS A SAD ONE.

"ONE DAY, LONG AGO...

"...A TRIO OF SIRENS SET UPON A VILLAGE."

"THEY USED THEIR MAGICAL SONG TO...

"... CONTROL THE VILLAGERS...

"...INCITE RAGE..."

DON'T LOOK AT ME LIKE THAT!

OR WHAT?!

BBBNNNGGG

"...AND CAUSE FIGHTING.

"WHICH THE SIRENS CONSUMED TO FUEL THEIR POWER."

"STYGIAN WAS A PONY LIKE THE REST OF US..."

OH NO!

"...THOUGH MORE SCHOLAR THAN HERO.

"HE RECOGNIZED OUR EMERGING WORLD WOULD NEED CHAMPIONS TO DEFEND IT."

LEAVE THEM ALONE!

CAN YOU CATCH ME?

AS SOMNAMBULA FLEW ABOVE, STARSWIRL USED HIS MAGIC...

ZORP!

ZXZXZXZRRRWNNNN

...OPENING A PORTAL FOR SOMNABULA TO USE AS A TRAP.

SHE AVOIDED IT AT THE LAST SECOND...

ZXZXZXZRRRN NNNN

...AND THE SIRENS FLEW RIGHT INTO THE VOID.

FWWWOOOOHHH!!!

VZP!

TRAPPED FOREVER.

"HE MAY HAVE GATHERED US TOGETHER...

"...BUT HE, HIMSELF, WAS JUST AN ORDINARY UNICORN...

"...WHO SOON GREW JEALOUS OF OUR ABILITIES.

"HE STOLE OBJECTS FROM EACH OF US...

"...OBJECTS TO USE IN A SPELL."

STYGIAN, WHAT IS THE MEANING OF ALL THIS?

"WE HAD NO CHOICE."

YOU CAN'T!

"WE CAST HIM OUT FOR IT.

"WE ALWAYS THOUGHT HE'D RETURN AND SEEK FORGIVENESS.

BWAAM

"BUT WHEN WE SAW HIM AGAIN..."

"...HIS HEART WAS BENT ON REVENGE."

GWAHHHH!!!

GWAH-

BWAH HA HA HA

"HE DASHED EVEN MY HOPE OF SAVING HIM."

STYGIAN?

ZOR-T-! VIP!

ZORTT!

BUT WHY DID HE STEAL THE ARTIFACTS FROM YOU?

NO DOUBT IT WAS AN ENCHANTMENT TO TAKE OUR POWERS FOR HIMSELF.

I WONDER...

WOW...

SOON, IN TWILIGHT'S LIBRARY...

THAT LOOKS LIKE A *LOT OF* WORK.

IT IS WHAT MUST BE *DONE*, AND IT WOULD BE BEST IF WE WERE NOT *DISTURBED*.

STARLIGHT NOTES THE TONE.

I'M SORRY, STARLIGHT, BUT WE CAN'T STOP TO TALK...

...THE STAKES ARE TOO HIGH AND WE HAVE TO—

BANISH STYGIAN TO LIMBO. I GET IT.

WHO?

STYGIAN WAS THE NAME THE PONY OF SHADOWS GAVE UP...

...WHEN HE TURNED TO DARKNESS.

AND I'M JUST TRYING TO FIGURE OUT WHY.

ENVY.

SLAMM

HE WANTED MORE POWER THAN HE HAD...

...AND THAT DESIRE LED HIM DOWN A PATH FROM WHICH THERE IS NO RETURN.

I KNOW FROM EXPERIENCE THAT'S NOT ALWAYS TRUE.

TWILIGHT. WHEN THE MAP CALLED YOU SIX TO MY VILLAGE...

...IT WAS FOR A *FRIENDSHIP* PROBLEM.

ARE YOU SURE THIS IS DIFFERENT?

I GUESS I'M NOT—

STYGIAN WANTS TO DESTROY ALL THAT IS *GOOD* IN THIS WORLD.

THERE'S NO WAY TO BEFRIEND A PONY LIKE THAT.

I GUESS I'M *LUCKY* YOUR *IDOL* WASN'T AROUND WHEN YOU DECIDED TO BE MY FRIEND.

I MIGHT'VE BEEN *BANISHED* TO LIMBO TOO.

IN THE CAVE OF HARMONY...

I AM GLAD WE HAVE THE CHANCE TO SEE WHAT HAS GROWN...

...FROM OUR EFFORTS LONG AGO.

IT SEEMS A SHAME TO HARM IT.

A NECESSARY SACRIFICE.

WITH THE ELEMENTS' POWER, WE WILL BIND THE PONY OF SHADOWS INTO LIMBO.

AND THANKS TO TWILIGHT, WE WILL REMAIN TO WATCH OVER THE REALM OURSELVES.

VORT!!

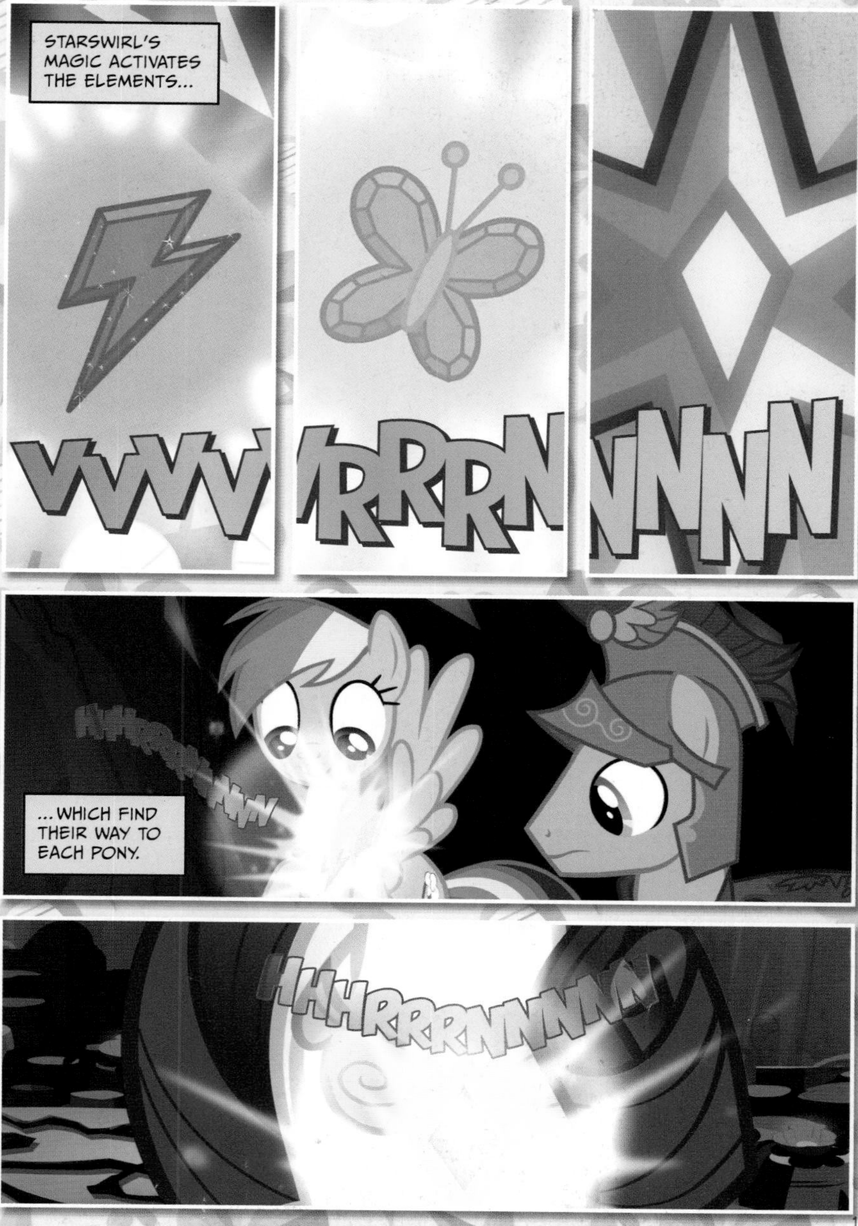
STARSWIRL'S MAGIC ACTIVATES THE ELEMENTS...
VVVVVRRRNNNNNN
HHHRRRNNNNN
...WHICH FIND THEIR WAY TO EACH PONY.
HHHRRRNNNNNN

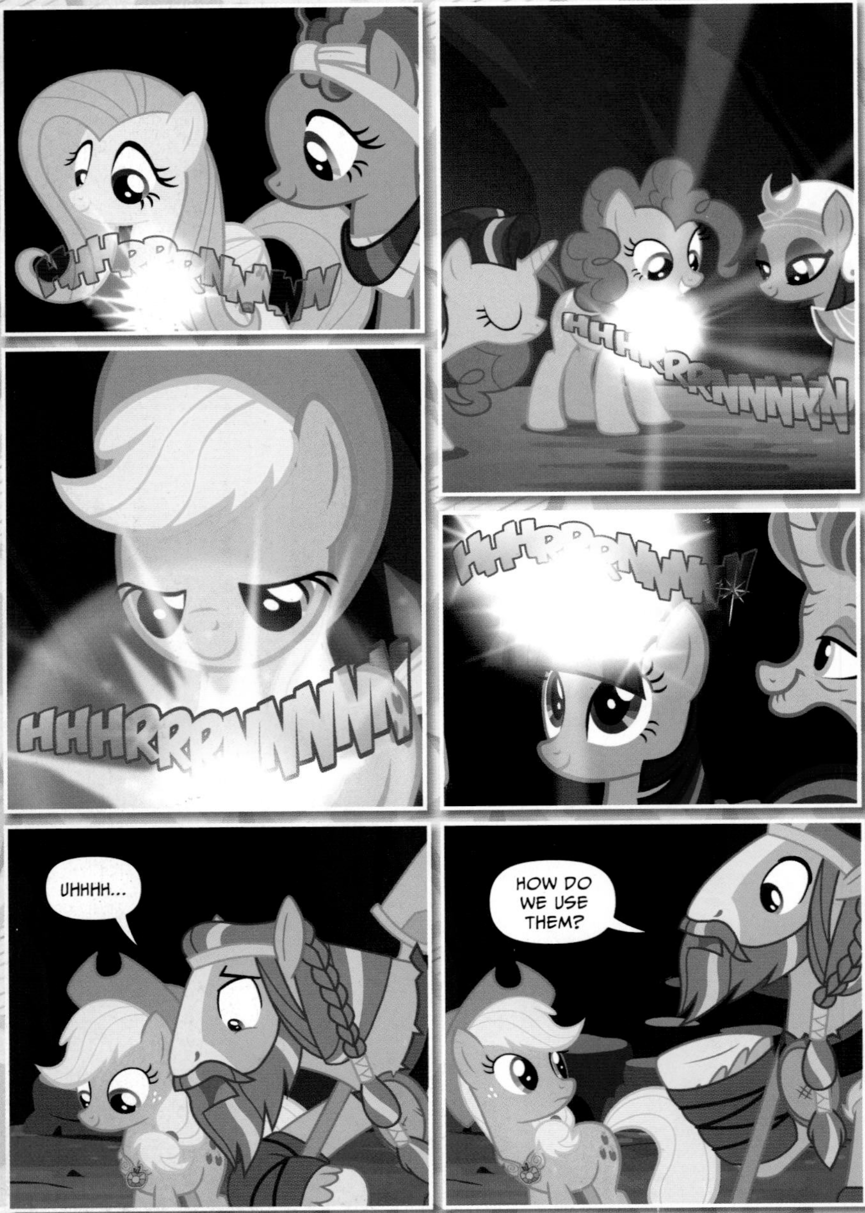
HHHRRRNNNNN
HHHRRRNNNNNN
HHHRRRNNNNNN
HHHRRRNNNNNN
UHHHH...
HOW DO WE USE THEM?

OH, I'M NOT SURE. THEY SIMPLY WORK FOR US.

THE ELEMENTS ARE ATTUNED TO YOU.

WE MUST USE THEIR MAGIC IN PAIRS.

NO PROBLEM.

WE'RE USED TO BANISHING EVIL BEFORE BREAKFAST.

AND IT'LL BE AN HONOR TO SAVE *EQUESTRIA* WITH Y'ALL.

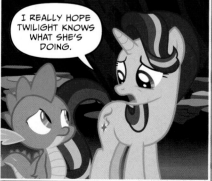

I REALLY HOPE TWILIGHT KNOWS WHAT SHE'S DOING.

LATER THAT SAME DAY...

I DON'T REMEMBER READING ANYTHING...

...THAT SAID THE *HOLLOW SHADES* WAS LIKE THIS.

THE PONY OF SHADOWS MUST HAVE *TWISTED* IT TO HIS PURPOSES.

PREPARE YOURSELVES.

HE IS HERE.

STYGIAN! SHOW YOURSELF AND FACE US!

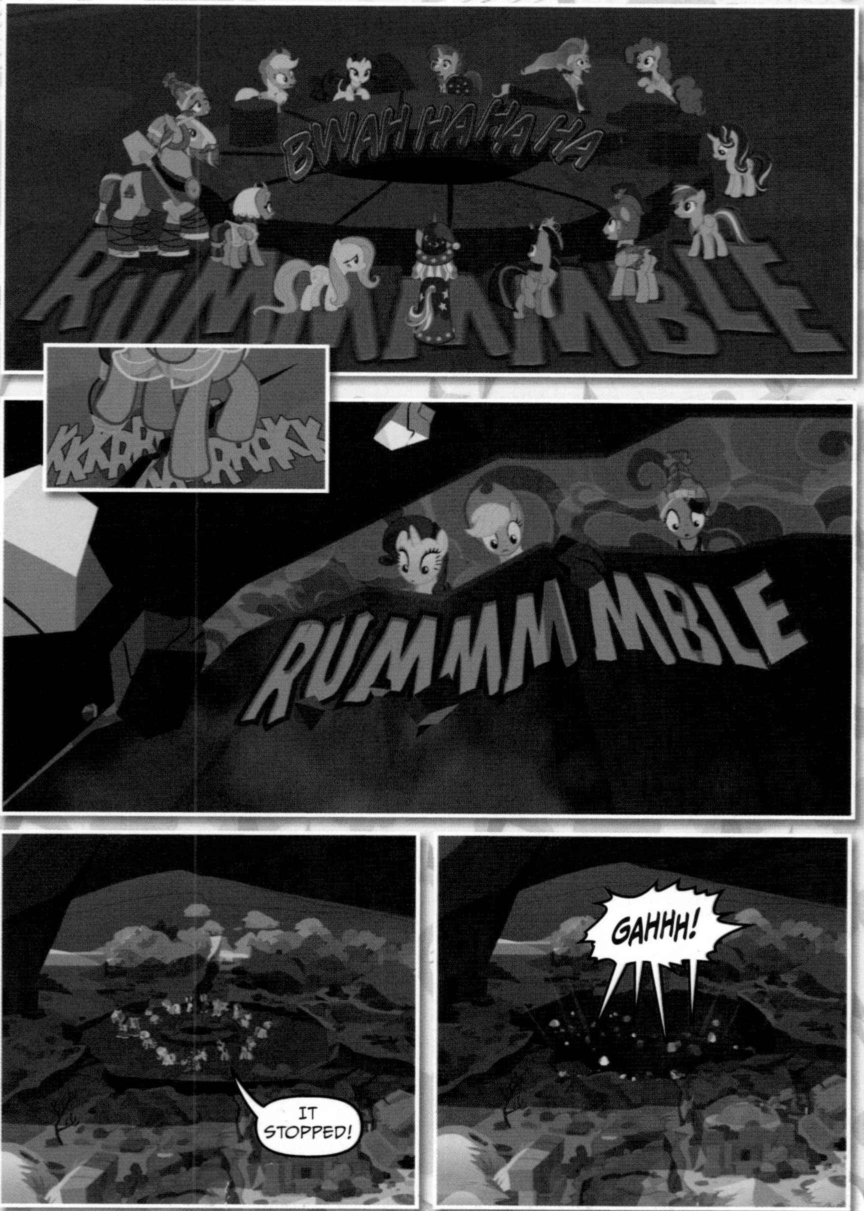
BWAH HA HA HA HA
RUMMMMBLE
IT STOPPED!
GAHHH!

CHAAM!

WHERE ARE WE?

I DEFINITELY WOULD HAVE REMEMBERED...

...READING ABOUT THIS PLACE—

BWAH HA HA HA

STARSWIRL QUICKLY PROTECTS THE GROUP.

BWAH HA HA HA

BWAH HA HA HA

WELCOME TO THE WELL OF SHADE.

WHEN YOU TURNED YOUR BACKS ON ME...

...I DISCOVERED THIS PLACE.

THE DARKNESS SPOKE TO ME OF A POWER BEYOND ANY I COULD IMAGINE.

AND I LISTENED.

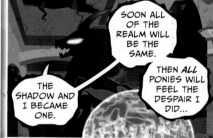

THE SHADOW AND I BECAME ONE.

SOON ALL OF THE REALM WILL BE THE SAME.

THEN *ALL* PONIES WILL FEEL THE DESPAIR I DID...

...WHEN YOU CAST ME OUT!

WE DID WHAT WE HAD TO DO. YOU TOOK OUR ARTIFACTS.

YOU TRIED TO STEAL OUR POWERS FOR YOURSELF.

NO! IT WAS YOU WHO WERE SELFISH.

NOW YOU WILL PAY!

VORTTT!!

KRRIIIPP

ARE YOU STILL SURE THIS ISN'T A FRIENDSHIP PROBLEM?

READY?! OPEN THE PORTAL!

VORTT!

ZZZXXXORTT!!!

NOW!

VVVWRRRNNNNN

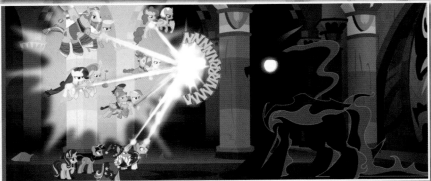

THE PORTAL OPENS!

YAAARRRRGH!

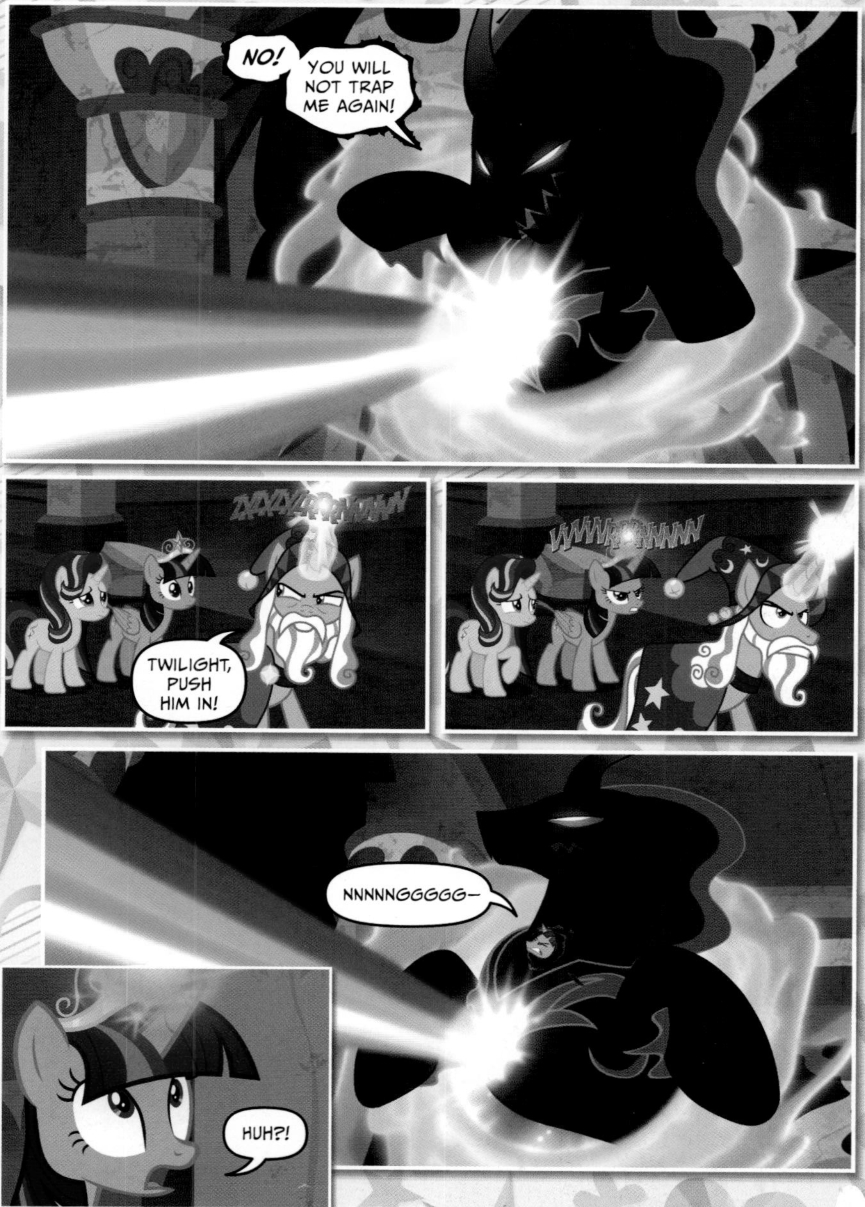
NO!
YOU WILL NOT TRAP ME AGAIN!
TWILIGHT, PUSH HIM IN!
NNNNNGGGGG—
HUH?!

HHHNNNNNGGGGG—

THERE'S A PONY IN THERE!

YAAARRRRGH!

BLAXXXRRRRTTTT!

FWAP!

VWWWRRRNNNNNN

ARE YOU... STYGIAN?

I WAS, ONCE.

UNTIL MY FRIENDS BETRAYED ME.

BUT STARSWIRL SAYS YOU BETRAYED *THEM*.

YOU WANTED THEIR MAGIC...

NO! I WANTED THEIR *RESPECT*.

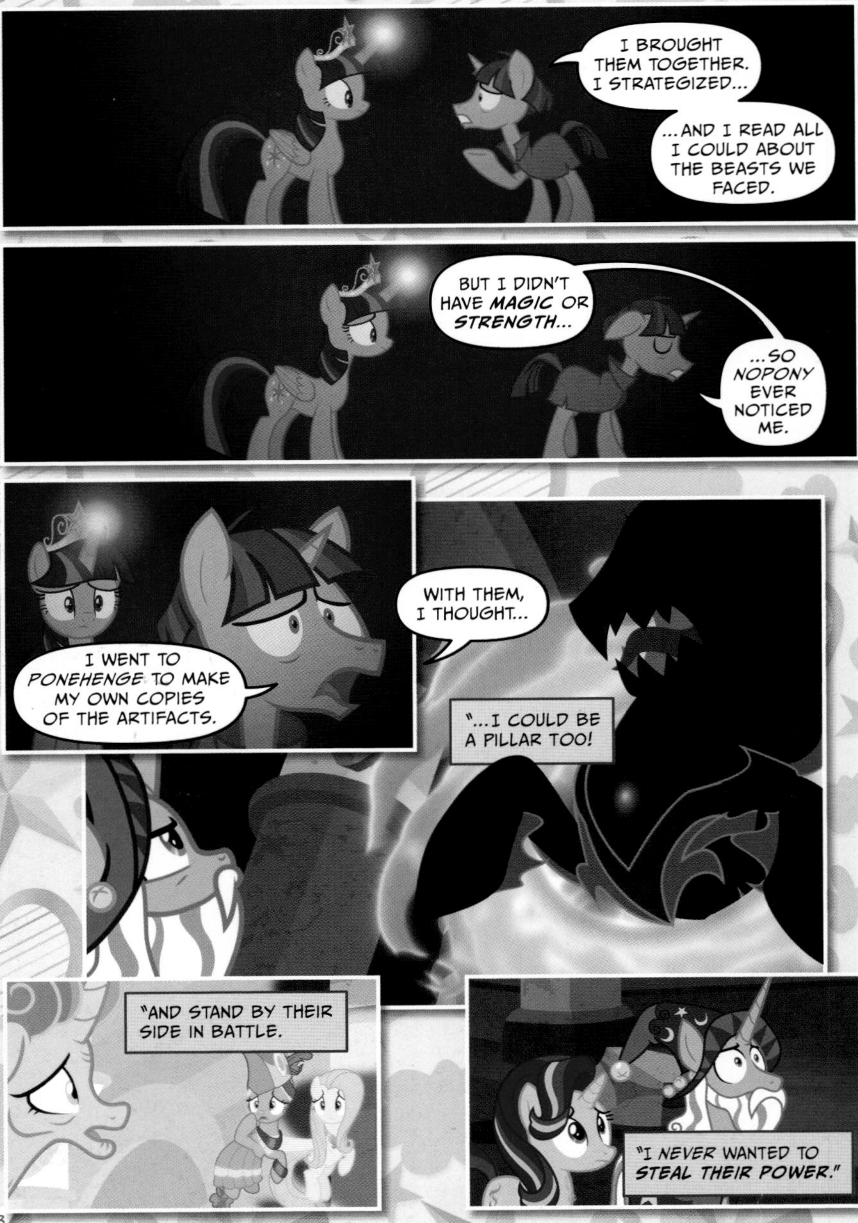
I BROUGHT THEM TOGETHER. I STRATEGIZED...
...AND I READ ALL I COULD ABOUT THE BEASTS WE FACED.
BUT I DIDN'T HAVE *MAGIC* OR *STRENGTH*...
...SO *NOPONY* EVER NOTICED ME.
I WENT TO *PONEHENGE* TO MAKE MY OWN COPIES OF THE ARTIFACTS.
WITH THEM, I THOUGHT...
"...I COULD BE A PILLAR TOO!
"AND STAND BY THEIR SIDE IN BATTLE.
"I *NEVER* WANTED TO *STEAL THEIR POWER.*"

BUT INSTEAD OF SHARING AND LETTING ME HELP...

...MY *FRIENDS* THREW ME OUT.

SO I BECAME *STRONGER* THAN ANY OF THEM!

THE DARKNESS WELCOMED ME WHEN *NOPONY* WOULD...

...AND I WILL DO WHAT I MUST TO PROTECT IT!

THIS IS ALL A MISUNDERSTANDING!

ZZZXXXXRRRRTTTT

"IF THE PILLARS KNEW HOW YOU FELT...

"...I'M SURE THEY WOULDN'T HAVE TURNED THEIR BACKS ON YOU."

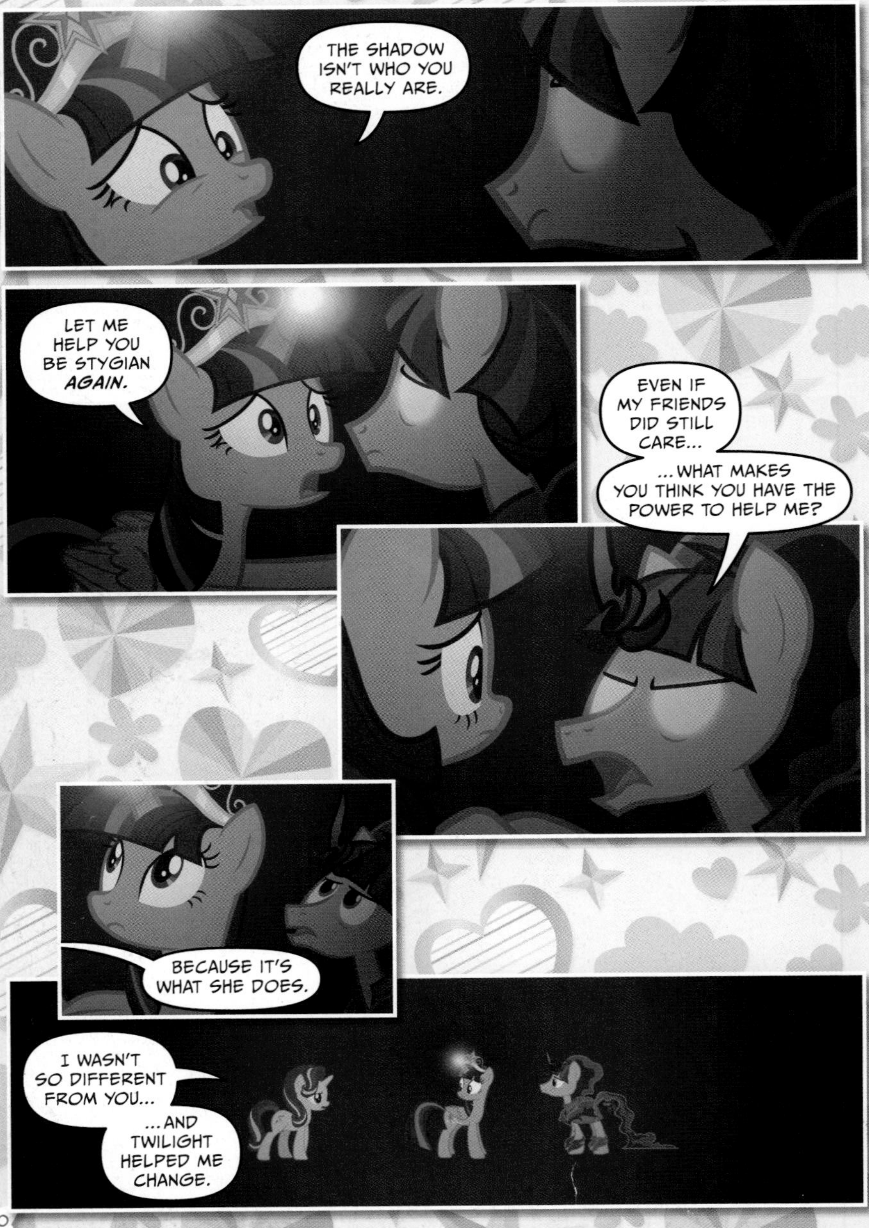
THE SHADOW ISN'T WHO YOU REALLY ARE.
LET ME HELP YOU BE STYGIAN *AGAIN.*
EVEN IF MY FRIENDS DID STILL CARE...
...WHAT MAKES YOU THINK YOU HAVE THE POWER TO HELP ME?
BECAUSE IT'S WHAT SHE DOES.
I WASN'T SO DIFFERENT FROM YOU...
...AND TWILIGHT HELPED ME CHANGE.

IF THERE'S ONE PONY IN EQUESTRIA THAT CAN SAVE A FRIENDSHIP, IT'S HER.

I WANT TO BELIEVE YOU.

BUT THE DARKNESS WILL NOT BE STOPPED!

UNGH!

VVVVURRRNNN!

ZORT!

YANK!

TWILIGHT GETS A MAGIC LINE AROUND STYGIAN'S HOOF.

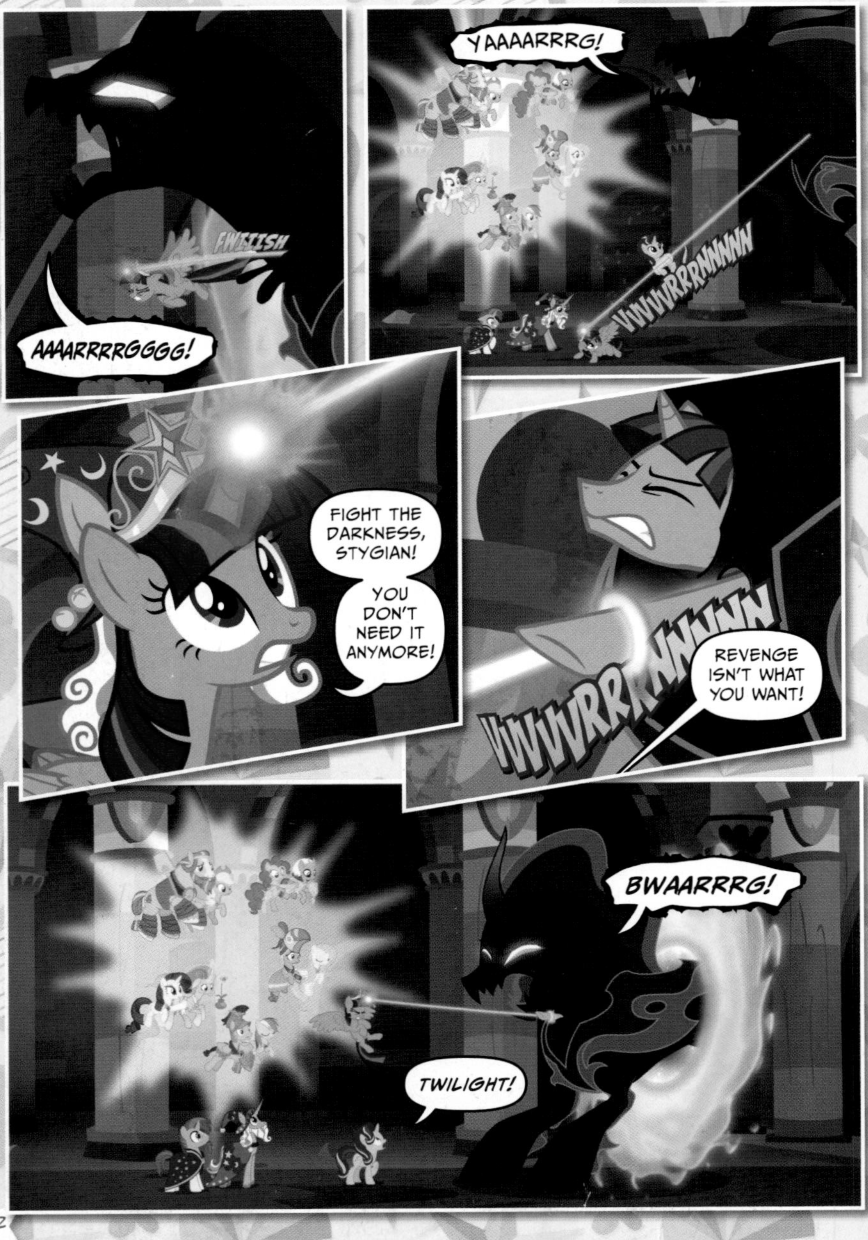

FWIIISH
AAAARRRRGGGG!
YAAAARRRG!
VVVVVRRRNNNNN
FIGHT THE DARKNESS, STYGIAN!
YOU DON'T NEED IT ANYMORE!
VVVVVRRRNNNNN
REVENGE ISN'T WHAT YOU WANT!
BWAARRRG!
TWILIGHT!

VORT!!

VVVUURRRNNNNN

THE SHADOW WON'T LET GO OF HIM!

HE WANTS TO STOP...

...BUT HE CAN'T DO IT ALONE.

THEN WE MUST HELP HIM.

ZIPD!

ZORT!

WWWWRRRRNNNNN

EVERYPONY, PULL!

NOOOOOOOOOO-
NOOOOOOOOOOOO-
KRAKABOOM

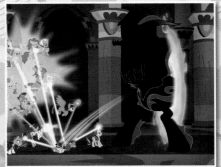

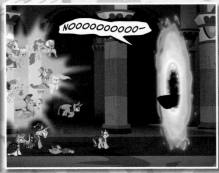

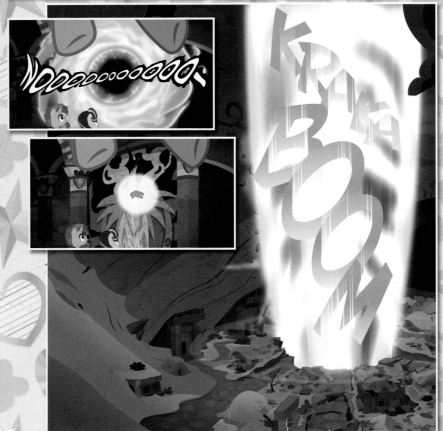

MOMENTS LATER...

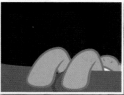

FWISH

WELL *THAT* WAS SOMETHING.

YEAH! IT FELT *SO GOOD* TO DO THAT AGAIN!

THE ELEMENTS!

THEY DIDN'T DISAPPEAR.

MAYBE BECAUSE WE USED THEM FOR *HEALING* MAGIC INSTEAD OF *BANISHING*?

LOOK!

HMPF!

LONG AGO YOU NEEDED OUR HELP, STYGIAN.

BUT INSTEAD OF LISTENING, WE TURNED OUR BACKS ON YOU.

PRIDE CLOUDED MY JUDGEMENT.

I OWE YOU AN APOLOGY.

THANK YOU FOR HELPING US SEE THE ERRORS OF OUR WAYS, TWILIGHT.

IT SEEMS I NEVER ACCOUNTED FOR...

...THE MAGIC OF FRIENDSHIP

THANK YOU, STARSWIRL.

SO... APPARENTLY A CONVERSATION CAN SAVE EQUESTRIA.

SOMETHING TELLS ME I WILL BE MAKING *A LOT* OF APOLOGIES TODAY.

BACK IN CANTERLOT...

I SIMPLY CANNOT BELIEVE HOW TALL YOU'VE GOTTEN!

WELL, IT HAS BEEN OVER A *THOUSAND* YEARS.

WILL YOU STAY HERE AND TEACH MAGIC ONCE AGAIN?

MY SISTER AND I HAVE FOND MEMORIES OF YOUR LESSONS.

AS LONG AS YOU DON'T ASK FOR THOSE ESSAYS WE OWED YOU...

...BEFORE YOU *DISAPPEARED.*

I AM NOT CERTAIN *CANTERLOT* IS WHERE I BELONG.

BUT THE REALM HAS GROWN...

...AND I THINK I'LL LOOK AROUND BEFORE SETTLING DOWN IN ANY ONE PLACE.

AND I LONG TO SEE WHAT HAS BECOME OF MY HOME.

I BELIEVE WE ALL DO.

...AND SHARE THE WISDOM OF YOUR GREAT EXPERIENCE WITH THE NEXT GENERATION OF PONIES.

THEN I HOPE YOU WILL RETURN TO CANTERLOT ON OCCASION...

WE WOULD BE HONORED.

BUT IF IT IS WISDOM YOU SEEK, LOOK NO FURTHER THAN YOUR OWN PUPIL.

SHE SHOWED ME THAT THE *POWER* OF *FRIENDSHIP* IS A MAGICAL FORCE INDEED.

AND THAT IN TURNING AWAY FROM OTHERS...

...YOU HURT YOURSELF AS WELL.

SQUEEEEZE

IT'S FUNNY. I THOUGHT MEETING MY IDOL WOULD GIVE ME ALL THE ANSWERS I EVER WANTED.

BUT INSTEAD, I FORGOT WHAT I ALREADY KNEW.

GOOD THING I HAD A STUDENT OF MY OWN TO REMIND ME.

NOT THE END!